THE BRIG

The Brig

by Mason Powell

the Outbound Press INC.

New York

The Brig
by Mason Powell

First Outbound Press Edition 1995

ISBN 0-9640291-1-1

Manufactured in the United States of America

Cover art by Nick Burkett

Published by The Outbound Press, Inc.
89 Fifth Avenue, Suite 803
New York, NY 10003

AUTHOR'S FOREWORD

What was life like for a boy growing up in the U.S. during the Vietnam war?

It was like living on a steady diet of fear. Fear as thick and palpable as cold oatmeal, served in portions big enough to choke you. Fear, promoted by politicians, fed to you from the first broadcast or newspaper of the morning. You woke up, the TV was turned on, and there was The War. At school all classes had an undertone of The War, even if it was viewed obliquely. On the radio songs were filled with The War.

Boys could look forward to graduating from high school and going right into one end of a meat grinder that would either spit them out as inedible or suck them in as Grade A meat and feed them into the target end of a shooting gallery. If they managed to get into college they might get a deferment; which only meant the sausage machine held off a while, waiting for them to get a degree before turning them into War fodder.

It is very hard to convey to young people today how pervasive that fear was. Boys lived with the conviction that they would, in all likelihood, have to fight in a bitter and incomprehensible war in a jungle somewhere in Asia, and that the war could escalate into something that could destroy the world, or at least all recognizable life.

Because of course there was more than just fear of the inexorable Draft to crush a young man's spirit. There was another heavy fear, a kind of mega-fear: the Bomb, the atomic and hydrogen bomb, an already loaded warhead, with your home town, or one nearby, as its sure target. The school air raid exercises of the 50s, so ludicrous in their meaningless ineffectiveness, had been dropped; everybody knew, deep down inside, that there was no place to run from Atomic War. One clutched at straws and hoped against hope that it would not happen, but it was always a possibility, always a dark angel waiting at your shoulder from the moment you became conscious of the world.

Meanwhile The War continued, and it lasted so long that many young people who died in it never knew a world in which it hadn't been going on.

The Brig is a real story, based upon real events that happened to a real human being.

Kelson, my partner for eighteen years, was indeed incarcerated in the brig for objecting to the war and brutally used by his Marine guards. Much of the book is fiction, but the scenes in the room with the wooden table are mostly what happened to him. He considered that they *did* break him. I had known him for some years before he was able to speak about his experiences, and I believe they haunted him to some degree to the day of his death, of AIDS.

Kelson was not the kind of boy you would have expected ever to find himself in a brig. He grew up in northern Wisconsin, in a large, devout Byzantine Catholic family. He was a middle child, and his early life was not much different from that of other kids in that time and place.

Well, maybe it was a little different.

Even as a very young child, Kelson felt he had a deeply religious vocation. When other boys and girls were playing store or doctor, he was talking his brothers and sisters into playing Mass. I treasure a snapshot of one Easter celebration in which a seven year-old Kelson, as the crucified Christ, stands in front of a makeshift cross, his golden curls framing a brightly smiling face.

He was not only a religious boy; he was also fervently patriotic. George Washington was his boyhood hero, he could never read enough about the American Revolution, and he delighted in historical recreations of Revolutionary War battles. One of the proudest moments of his childhood (which he continued to treasure to the end of his life) came when he was allowed to carry the American flag and lead the Fourth of July parade in his home town… and dressed in a Superman costume, to boot!

Except that he wanted to become a priest, he considered himself and was considered by others just a typical, ordinary American teenager (he didn't really understand that the deep love he bore his best male friend in high school was anything out of the ordinary). It's true he was more pious and patriotic than some, but all in all he was definitely not the kind of boy you'd think destined to land in the brig.

After high school he entered a seminary, but left before he had completed his first year. His faith was powerful, but he had a probing mind, and asked too many questions about matters which he couldn't accept on faith, to the annoyance of his teachers. At loose ends, he joined the Navy.

All of which is so far pretty much the biography of the young sailor in my novel.

I think it's important to say here that Kelson loved the Navy, that he loved military life, loved all the things he learned in it (he became a proficient metal caster), loved his shore leaves in exotic ports (he got engaged to a Puerto Rican girl and probably would have married her if things had worked out differently), loved the coffee houses where the sailors hung out and where enlisted men held poetry readings.

That last is important, too. Unlike the Second World War—everybody's model for a clearcut war in which good battled evil—the Vietnam Era did not take place in black and white. It was a time of great contradiction and paradox. There was nothing strange about a coffee house full of military personnel holding anti-war poetry readings. Very few people had unequivocal, all or nothing, feelings about the war. The only thing that unified everybody in the United States of America was the desire that the war be over. Just how that was to be accomplished was the national bone of contention.

Kelson found himself editing a poetry magazine out of the coffee house, and becoming increasingly disenchanted with military authoritarianism, which required the same sort of unquestioning belief that he had been unable to accept in the seminary. He became more and more convinced that the Vietnam War was wrong, and that he could no longer in good conscience continue to participate in it.

He wasn't a man to chain himself to a fence, however, or lie down in the path of trucks delivering munitions. He didn't want to be a trouble-maker. He was an ordinary man who believed in following rules, so he simply went to his superiors, explained his position, and tried to deal with the matter through the official channels available to him.

It might have worked. After all, Kelson was not the first man to join the military and want out, nor the last—for that time and place, actions like his were not even unusual; there were so many similar cases, in fact, that they'd become an embarrassment to the government, and to the military in particular; procedures had even been specially developed to handle them. If things had gone as they should have, Kelson might have been able to effect a gentler separation from the Navy. The doctor aboard his ship was working with him to secure his discharge, and Kelson was doing his part to help speed things along by writing his congressman. That congressman, by the way, is still in office.

Things went wrong. Kelson got sick, ran a high fever and needed to see the doctor. But the doctor who was helping him was off ship, and the man who replaced him that night was not sympathetic. He sent Kelson back to work, and the work was loading bombs. It all came together in one of those moments that *should* have been avoided, but... Well, that's why I wrote a book called *The Brig*.

For Kelson,
Whose Misfortunes
Inspired it:
With Love, Rather
Than with pain,
Because I think he'll
Like it more.

One

I was straight, and that was one thing I was sure of. I had a girl that I was almost engaged to, and that proved something, didn't it? Even if she and I hadn't gone all the way; well, she wasn't that kind of girl! I had no doubt whatsoever that I was straight, and no two ways about it!

I was almost as sure of that as I was that the war in 'Nam was a crock of shit and that I couldn't, wouldn't, in any good conscience, take any part in it. — Or in any kind of killing and maiming and butchery.

Well then, what was I doing in the Navy?

That was a question I had asked myself again and again as I sat on my bunk, waiting for the commander of my ship to call for me. I was in the Navy, and what I was doing was against the tradition of the services for more than a hundred years. What would they do to me?

That question was the one I was really asking myself. Every guy who has ever been in the service has heard tales of what happens to men in the Brig. Most of the stories are as much a crock as the war. But there are some of them that persist, and some of them are scarier than others. That's why I was worried, not only what they would do to me on an official level, but what might happen not-so-officially. One of the guys aboard ship told me that he had been in the Brig, and that the only way to survive was to roll with the punches and swing whatever way they wanted you to swing.

That was fine for him to say! He made no bones about what he did at sea when there were no women around and there was nobody watching. But I was straight! And not only that, I was still, technically, a virgin—something nobody else on the ship knew, and that I didn't want to get around. I had a bad enough reputation for deciding, just when they were finished training me and ready to get some of their money back, to become a conscientious objector.

I sat there cursing myself for being the dumbest guy who ever lived, and probably the easiest to push around. My father had pushed me, my mother had pushed me, and instead of fighting back, I just did what seemed easiest at the time. But as I got older I got tired of it, and I started looking for a way out.

Now the average kid of sixteen would look for a job in a gas station, and when he found it, he would start looking for a place of his own. But not me! I decided to become a priest! And weren't my parents pleased?

They were not! They thought the world of all the priests in the world, but to have a son of theirs a celibate and not carry on the family name was going too far. That was the first real satisfaction I ever got out of them: the way they blew up when I told them I was going to do something they had always indicated would be a wonderful thing, not only for me, but for them.

But it got me away from home. There were ten states between me and my parents, and I thought it was paradise for the first two weeks. Then the old gonads started to ache, and I realized that for a boy just turning seventeen, masturbation is not only a necessity, it's a way of life. I coped as best I could, but my confessor got tougher and tougher on the penances, and I started to realize that not only wasn't I physically ready for the rigors of celibacy, I was beginning to doubt the whole theology that required it of me.

I held on for nearly a year at the seminary, but my body got stronger and my faith got weaker. It was a war between the father superior and me, and finally the old buzzard decided I wasn't worth the effort and kicked me out.

That left two alternatives. I could go home in shame, or I could find a job. Not being trained in anything but praying, jobs were scarce. My self-confidence was pretty low, too. That was why the big poster and the TV ads telling me how I could learn a trade and see the world in the Navy started looking attractive. Being dumb and easy to push, I joined.

And my parents, who were always so patriotic it made me want to puke, were they happy? They were not! They didn't figure they had raised a son just so he could go off and get killed! Why couldn't I have done like the boy down the street, and got the local Quakers to say I was a conscientious objector?

I realized, as I turned eighteen, that my parents were hypocrites. Worse, that practically everybody was. And worse than that, that I wasn't and had no desire to be.

The Navy started out pretty good for me. I liked boot camp in San Diego, and I started to take an interest in my body, which I now realized was pretty good. 'A swimmer's body,' one of my instructors called it. And when I got out of boot camp, I found it was easy to throw myself into learning my new career. I was training aboard a destroyer tender to be a molder, and the smell of hot steel and other molten metals was one I liked.

I made petty officer, third class before my good old conscience got in the way. By that time I had enough free time that I could watch the news and read the papers; and what I saw appalled me. World War II was one thing: napalming little kids was another. I ended up hanging around with a vociferous anti-war crowd aboard ship, a new phenomenon in the Navy of those days; and before I knew it, I was marked as a troublemaker.

Even so, on my own I would probably have never done anything more than gripe if it hadn't been for a party one Saturday night. I got so drunk that I made a speech about how we should all quit, and somebody talked me into putting in for a discharge to see if it would work. I didn't even remember the letter until the Old Man called me in, livid and wanting to know what the hell I thought I was doing.

And even then I could have got out of it just by apologizing and withdrawing the letter and saying it was something I'd done when I was drunk.

But the Old Man was a lot of things rolled up into one. He looked a lot like my father, and he talked a lot like the father superior at the seminary, and something in me just would not knuckle under one more time. I got mad, and I told him I was sticking to my guns, and that tore it.

The next month was hell on water. I pulled extra watches at odd hours. I got extra duties that I knew damn well should have gone to somebody else. Finally I got the flu, and even the doctor said I should be in bed. But the Old Man continued his persecutions, and one night, in a fever, I walked off a watch.

Slam! I was under arrest and confined to quarters until they decided what to do with me.

In desperation I wrote a letter to my congressman, that being the only thing I could think of. Hal Rosenblum was at that time considered the nation's hope by the New Left. He was a vigorous campaigner for civil rights and he had spoken openly in Congress against the war. I figured if anybody could help me, he could!

But once the letter was mailed, my last bolt was shot! I knew the military regulations well enough to know that if I persisted I would get my discharge, and that it would be honorable. But how long would I have to persist? And what would I have to go through first?

My answer came too soon.

A message arrived that the Old Man wanted to see me in his quarters in half an hour sharp.

Well, this is it! I thought. Then I realized I was soaking wet with perspiration. I grabbed a dress uniform and headed down to the showers, figuring that it wouldn't be much of a grandstand if I arrived looking like a drowned dog.

The water cooled me off and restored a little of my calm. As I dressed I checked myself out in the mirror, making sure I was shaved and all that.

I was a pretty good-looking kid, I estimated. Blond, with blue eyes. A grin that more than one girl had told me was nice. That 'swimmer's body;' not bulging with muscles, but compact and solid and well-proportioned. I had a nice mat of hair on the upper part of my chest, from just below the nipples on up to the hollow of my throat. A fine line of hair went down the middle of my not-quite-washboard stomach and spread out below my navel into a luxuriant but soft bush around my genitals. My cock was not the biggest one on board ship; but it wasn't small either, and my balls hung down nicely below it. I figured that some day my almost-fiancé would have a tough time taking it!

I dressed and headed up to the officer's quarters, and tried to keep my mind off whatever might be coming.

Something turned over in my stomach when I walked in and closed the door behind me. The Old Man was seated behind his desk looking at some papers, but there were three Marines in the room as well: military police, all decked out to the teeth with weapons sticks and leather, and that bothered me. If there is anything in the world a sailor doesn't enjoy seeing, it's a Marine M.P.

We went through the usual formalities; then the Old Man got right down to business.

"I've got two pieces of paper in front of me," he said. "One of them is a form all made out in your name, requesting that your request for discharge be dropped. If you sign it, you'll finish your hitch just the way you signed up for, and that will be that. If you refuse to sign it, we'll have to go through the whole procedure of the discharge, and during that time you will be remanded to the custody of these men and live in the Brig, ashore. — That's what the other piece of paper is; the orders turning you over to them."

"Thank you, Sir," I said, "but I still want the discharge."

The Old Man leaned back in his chair and fixed me with a look that sent chills up my spine. It wasn't precisely malevolent, but there was evil in it; and, what really shook me up, there was humor in it too!

"Before you make that decision," he said, "I want you to know just what it entails. These men are not just military police. They are a special force carefully trained to deal with cases like yours. It will be eight weeks minimum before all the paperwork on your discharge comes through. During that time you will be totally in their keeping. This country has had your kind before. We haven't lasted this long without learning how to deal with them!"

My heart had begun to pound, and I had flashes running across my mind of all the horror stories that I had ever heard of the Brig. But if I gave in now, I realized, the rest of my hitch would be almost as bad as whatever they had planned for me. I could not imagine at that moment that the United States Government would allow anything really monstrous to happen in its prisons. —But I was pretty young, and pretty stupid!

"Sergeant," the Old Man said, "tell this boy what he should do."

The Marine sergeant was standing immediately to my left and a little closer to the Old Man than I was, so I could see his face clearly as he stood in place and spoke. He and the two corporals with him were all a head taller than I was, and they had broad shoulders and muscles that bulged through their uniforms. Their physical stature alone was intimidating, but the cruel smile that played about the sergeant's lips as he spoke, the glint in his jet black eyes, and the depth and security of his powerful voice were terrifying. He didn't raise his deep voice, but almost whispered as he spoke.

"You should sign the form, and go back to being a petty officer, third class. It'll break you, and you'll know you've been broken; but you'll still be able to call yourself a man after you get out. If you get turned over to us, you'll not only get broken, you'll lose whatever right to call yourself a man you have. That conscience that you value so highly will go right down the drain."

What the sergeant said wasn't a threat; it was a promise. He didn't say it like a man planning to do something. He said it like a man who has done it, over and over. I swallowed, and I thought they must all be able to hear my heart pounding.

But it wouldn't do any good to pull out now, I told myself. It was the difference between eight weeks of hell and three years of it. If I could last through whatever they had in mind, I would be out, for once and for all. Further, I could tell the world about it. Let that fall down around their ears!

"I'd still like my discharge, Sir!" I said.

I was frightened, sure! Who wouldn't be? But competing inside me with the fear was something else. I naively half-imagined myself to be like the freedom riders who were putting their lives on the line in Georgia and Mississippi. Like the demonstrators who were matching their passive resistance against the lines of troops trying to get in and out of Port Chicago. Whatever happened to me, I knew there would be a hero's welcome when I got out, and I would be able to strike a tremendous blow for justice!

How stupid can a kid get?

The Old Man signed the papers, the sergeant signed some papers for him, and I marched out behind the sergeant and the two corporals on my way to the Brig.

Nobody spoke until we got to the military prison, a grey, crumbling cement building that was probably put up during World War I, and which should have been torn down before Pearl Harbor. I was marched into an office where a Marine lieutenant looked over my papers, then swore under his breath.

"Shit! A God-damned conshy!"

He looked at the sergeant, then looked me up and down with disgust.

"I hope you boys have fun with him!" he said.

There were more formalities; then I was marched into another room with a stack of strongboxes on one side and a lot of shelves stacked with clothing on the other.

"Strip!" the sergeant said.

I did as I was told and the man behind the counter took all my clothes, except my boots, and all my valuables, filled out a form describing them, got me to sign it, then locked everything in one of the strongboxes. He asked me my sizes, then fetched prison clothing for me. A pair of socks, a pair of dungarees, a pair of standard boxer shorts, and a white teeshirt with BRIG stenciled on the back in big, black block letters.

"Put those on!" the sergeant ordered, still in that menacing, quiet voice, but with the snap of a drill sergeant in it.

I dressed and we marched out.

Past a couple of cell blocks where about fifteen men each were imprisoned. Past a row of cells with one or two men each. Past some cells where there was only one man each. Then, out of the area with open cells and down a long, long corridor with just steel doors on either side.

We turned a corner, went through a door, and were in an open, galvanized metal shower room. There were only three showers, and on one side there was a laundry bin, on the other a shelf with towels and clothing.

"Strip!" the sergeant said again. "And throw your dirty clothes in that bin!"

I almost laughed. It seemed such a stupid thing. I had just put on the fresh clothes. But there are three ways of doing things, and the military way is the dumbest.

Then it occurred to me that what I was about to get might not be a shower. This was a distant, and as far as I could tell, an empty part of the building. My mouth went dry.

"I just put these on..." I stammered, but the sergeant cut me off.

"Shut up!" he said softly. "And when you speak to me, if you ever have reason to speak to me, first say: 'Sir! Yes, Sir!', and when you've finished speaking, say, 'Sir,' again."

He had that damned smile on his lips, and suddenly I was mad as hell.

I smiled back at him, my most boyish, irrepressible grin, and said: "Sergeant, I'm not sure I quite remember the way the ranks work, but is a Marine sergeant superior to a Navy petty officer, third class?"

His smile didn't waver, but he gestured to indicate our surroundings.

"Here it is," he said. "Now strip!"

I did as I was told, terrified, wondering what they were going to do to me. As soon as I had my clothes off, however, one of the corporals turned on the water, told me to adjust it myself, then all three stepped back and the sergeant told me to shower.

I thought at that moment it was the scariest shower I'd ever had. More so than the one at camp, when I was a kid, where you had to do it in the dark for an initiation and they told you there were snakes that hung around under the showers. I finished, took a towel, and dried myself off. As I finished, a bundle of clothes hit me in the face and the sergeant told me to dress again, and then we marched off again, deeper into the dim corridors of the prison.

The last corridor we came to had no doors at the sides, only one at the end, and it was to this one that I was taken. It was a steel door with a little steel window in it and a trap at the bottom for sliding food in. There were bolts at three places on it, and the sergeant opened it for me to go in.

"This is where you'll live for the next eight weeks," he said. "You'll get three meals a day. The morning meal will be a little late, because you'll have a session with us before breakfast every day. Eat what they give you; you'll need it. And eat it when it comes, so you stay on schedule."

He stopped talking, so there was nothing else for me to do. I walked through the door into the cell. The door slammed behind me with a clang, and in a momentary flashback to my days at the seminary I thought: "I'm in the hands of the Inquisition!"

Two

The cell was small and had no windows. There was a ventilator in the ceiling, and a heat duct, and a fluorescent light behind glass that had wire in it, so it couldn't be broken. There was a cot with a pillow and blankets, and a sink with hot and cold water, and a toilet that had had the seat removed.

It wasn't as bad as I had imagined, but it wasn't the Ritz, either.

It had been morning when I left the ship and checked in at the Brig, so I figured the first meal they slid under the door was lunch. Actually, it looked more like the bilges with sawdust added, and that from me who had never been critical of military cooking; not after my mother! But I ate it, and it wasn't too bad. That is, it wasn't nasty. It was flavorless! A sort of porridge, with a glass of something that wasn't water, but wasn't anything else either, to drink.

I figured the first thing I would have to do was figure out how not to be bored between whatever ominous 'sessions' the sergeant had in mind for me. There was no one to talk to. There was nothing to read, not even on the white-washed walls. The room was even warm enough, so I couldn't pretend I was a monk in a cold monastery. I tried praying, but that turned out to be a bad idea. The only thing I ended up praying for was deliverance from the Brig, and that only served to strengthen my fears.

By suppertime I knew the boredom was going to be bad, so I tried to focus my interest on the food. But it was the same thing as lunch, only more of it. That was when I knew the boredom was going to be bad, and the food a major part of the boredom.

I lay down on my cot and decided that I would work on my talent for daydreaming. Every kid in the world gets told he's no good because he daydreams too much. Maybe this was my chance to make use of an otherwise useless talent!

After I'd gone through my whole life at least twice, I began to wonder when they were going to turn the lights off. And after I'd gone through my whole life ten more times, I realized they weren't going to. By then I was tired, so I went to sleep.

I was awakened by a churning in my guts and a very sudden call to nature. I got to the toilet and my lunch and dinner in a pretty much unchanged form, it seemed to me, exploded out of my ass. I always hated those kinds of sudden diarrhoeas, and cursed the cooks in the Brig, then the Marines, then the Old Man. When the siege was over I got back in bed and drew the covers up, but I was barely asleep when I heard the bolts of the door shot and the door opened.

"Get up!" the sergeant barked.

Had the whole night passed? Usually I was just about ready to get up when it was time to get up. Maybe the schedule at the Brig was different, I noted, climbing up, still dressed.

"Come on," the sergeant said, his voice now back to normal.

I left my cell and there I was, back between the same two corporals, behind the sergeant, marching down the grey corridors. They took me to the shower room and once again I was required to strip and shower. But this time as I finished drying myself off, the sergeant said: "Look at me!"

He was standing directly in front of me, and I did as I was told.

"Parade rest!" he said.

I took the required position, hands behind my back, legs apart.

One of the corporals stepped on into the shower stall and turned on the water again. He adjusted it so that it poured down my back, the top of the spray hitting at my neck, the rest on my back and butt.

The water poured down for a long time, then I noticed that it was slowly getting hotter. The sergeant stood there in front of me, silent, with that damned smile playing on his lips and in his black eyes. The water got hotter and hotter. I knew now what the first game was gong to be, and I determined to beat it. I stared him straight in the eyes and held on as the water became scalding. My back, my hands, my ass, all were screaming with the pain of the searing water. Clouds of steam rose up all around me, and the sweat trickled down into my eyes and burned. But I wasn't going to give in!

Finally the sergeant nodded and the water stopped. The second corporal threw the towel at me and I nearly fumbled it, so great was the relief of not being burned anymore and so shaky was I. I was ordered to dry myself and dress, and then I was marched back to my cell, and the first ordeal was over.

But as I went through the door, the sergeant said as quietly as always: "Eight weeks!"

And with sudden and full comprehension, I understood what he meant. He didn't have to do anything with me quickly. He had eight full weeks in which to break me, and he meant to do it slowly and completely!

Breakfast was the same, and lunch was the same, and dinner was the same; and getting up the next morning with the runs was the same too, and that worried me. Were they going to feed me what the law required, but starve me to death by putting laxatives in it every day?

I didn't have time to think about it. The door opened and I was marched to the shower again.

Once more the shower, and once more the parade rest under the water that slowly got hotter and hotter until it was scalding. Then, when I thought I was going to pass out from the heat and the pain, the sergeant barked: "Ten-s*hun!* About *face!* Parade *rest!*"

And I, having been conditioned by military training, responded to the command without thinking, and there I was, the front of my body in the stream of scalding water, the fiery shower pouring down my chest, singeing my belly, and burning my cock and balls. Unable to deal with it, I cried out, and instantly the water stopped. I doubled over at the pain, clutching my balls, my mind gone for the moment in the sheer pain.

I heard the Marines chuckling quietly, but I didn't care. My balls hurt too much to care about anything. Then I heard the sergeant speak, and I felt the horror of panic.

"I said parade rest. I didn't give you permission to break. Corporal, bring the heat up slower this time."

There was nothing I could do. I was in the Brig. These men could do anything they wanted to me! But I realized, even as I stood up and assumed parade rest, that as long as my mind was my own, I would survive.

The water started, pouring down my chest, warm and pleasant. I looked at the shower as if it were a cobra spitting venom at me. The temperature increased. From the corner of my eye I could see the corporal who was ever so slowly turning the handle of the faucet. He was as young as I was, with very fair skin and freckles. His hair was red, and he looked like a farm boy. The smirk on his face didn't look evil. If I weren't his victim, I wouldn't have believed he were capable of torturing someone.

The water reached the scalding stage. I clenched my fists so tight I thought I must surely dig my nails right through my palms. My cock and balls had shrunk up almost completely inside me in a vain attempt to defend themselves from the boiling water. I thought that in another minute I would faint from the pain, but it went on, and then I thought maybe I would throw up.

Then it ended, and I stood shaking. When the towel hit me I was barely able to use it and I dressed myself in a daze, clumsy and quaking. They marched me back to my cell and put me in, and I fell onto the cot in a wave of nausea.

This was only my third day in the Brig, I thought, and they had already done this to me!

After a while the heat began to drain out of my body, and I started to shiver. I drew the covers up over me and tried to make myself pass out, but that was the moment when the detestable breakfast came through the slot in the door, clattering. I ignored it for a long time, but eventually my hunger roused me up and it occurred to me that there was one good thing about the water torture: when it was finished, your body threw it off fairly quick.

On the fourth day things got worse, for now the sergeant began his program of breaking me in earnest. I had imagined that I might get beaten up, or worked over with hoses, or forced to suck cock, or even raped. I was unprepared for the sergeant with his quiet voice, his smile, and his willingness to do everything slowly. I had been tortured for three days, and the only thing they'd used on me was water from the shower! I could never have imagined using a shower that way. What would the sergeant do next?

I found out.

First the shower, then the parade rest with scalding water. I knew it was coming this time, so I was able to hold up a little better. My balls still burned, and I was nearly ready to fall down when the water was finally turned off, but I hadn't doubled up with pain; so I figured I was holding my own.

I dried off and dressed and fell in between the two corporals and we marched off. But we didn't go back to my cell, and all the fear came flooding back.

We marched a long way through the grey corridors, past some of the cell blocks and finally entered a room in what I recognized as the prison hospital. There were all the usual paraphernalia and in the middle, the usual examination table.

A corpsman came in, a young man with brown hair and nondescript features.

"What can I do for you today?" he asked the sergeant.

"Got a prisoner we're working on," the sergeant said pleasantly. "Want him pre-opped."

The terror ran through me again, this time mingling with the pain in my body to intensify it.

"Sure," said the corpsman. "I'll get the stuff. Get him up on the table!"

My breathing was coming heavy now. Were they going to perform some kind of operation on me? Suddenly the sergeant's words came back to me about leaving less than a man.

"Sergeant," I began, but again he cut me off.

"Shut up! What did I tell you to say if you ever had to speak to me?"

It was no time to argue ranks.

"Sir! Yes, Sir!" I rapped, as smartly as I could with all the fear.

"Permission to speak granted," the sergeant said, obviously pleased with my response.

"Sir, if you're planning some kind of operation on me, I should warn you that I have written to certain high officials, and my death or bodily harm will be noted, Sir!"

For the first time, the sergeant broke out into a wide grin. He had perfect white teeth, and to me they made him look totally carnivorous.

"I do believe you are beginning to feel fear," he said. "That's good, because you have reason to be afraid. But I'm not going to perform any operations on you. Not the kind you think, at any rate. When you get out of here at the end of eight weeks, there won't be a physical mark on your body. Not a single trace of what's happened to you here. But you've heard how the Marine Corps builds men? Well, we also know how to tear them down. And that's something that happens to your soul, boy. And that leaves a lot of scars where they don't show. — Now do as I say! Strip, and get up on that table, face down."

Once more I did as I was told, a whole new wave of fear washing over me. Stories about Communists and their brain-washing techniques came into my mind.

The corpsman came back in.

"Where do you want him shaved?" he asked.

"From the neck down," said the sergeant.

"Okay," said the corpsman.

I felt the cold jelly smeared all over my body, and then I felt the brusque scraping of a razor. There was a patch of hair in the middle of my back just above my ass, and that went first. Then all the hair on my ass, and then on down my legs.

"Roll over!" the sergeant said.

I rolled over and the corpsman smeared the jelly all over my body again, this time smearing it between my legs and all over my cock and balls. He started by shaving my chest and belly, then went down to my legs, then finally got to my pubic hair.

"Spread your legs!" the sergeant said, and I did it.

I felt the harsh scrape of the razor moving down my bush, taking the pubic hair in big clumps, moving closer and closer to my cock. Then he held my cock between his fingers, pulled it away from my body, and shaved it outward, toward the head. Last he took the razor down between my legs and shaved upward from the base of my balls and all over my scrotum.

"There you go," he said. "All finished. I'd suggest you take him down to the showers and wash that soap off. It can be a little irritating if you leave it on the skin too long. Remember, when you shave, you cut off just a little of the outer layer of the epidermis."

"I don't think we have to worry about his skin getting too irritated," the sergeant chuckled. "Get up! Get dressed!"

I got up, dressed, and they marched me back to my cell. Once inside I took the corpsman's advice and rinsed myself off as best I could with the water from the sink; but as I went over my naked body, I was completely demoralized. I felt humiliated. It was almost like what I imagined rape to be like, or rather, what one felt afterwards. A man's body hair is one of the tokens of his masculinity. When they had talked about pre-op, I was afraid that I was in for castration. Now I realized that was just what was happening to me, only on a psychological level instead of physically.

The next morning was awful. My body burned and itched all over. I was all over razor burn. As they marched me to my rendezvous with the scalding shower I wondered if it was not better to give in now. As I stripped and showered, I contemplated the weeks ahead, and knew I couldn't go on.

"Sir! Yes, Sir!" I said when I finished my shower, standing at attention looking at the man who had brought me to this state of humiliation.

"Permission to speak granted," the sergeant said pleasantly.

"Sir!" I said. "I ... I ... I can't take it any more, Sir! I'll sign the other paper. I'll give up my discharge, Sir!"

There was a moment of silence, and I kept my eyes on the floor. I was ashamed at my weakness, I was humiliated, but I couldn't take it any longer. Then I heard laughter. Not just the sergeant, but the corporals, too, were laughing.

"Parade rest!" the sergeant said through his laughing.

"But, Sir," I said, "I'm willing to sign it!"

"It's too late," one of the corporals said with a drawl, the one with the red hair and the freckles. It was the first time I had heard either of them speak.

"You only get one chance," said the sergeant. "After that the machinery is in motion. The paper work grinds on and on. You can't take it back. And you have to go the whole course, once they assign you to us. Now, parade *rest!*"

I broke. I tried to run, naked as I was. I started screaming. But we were way in the back of the prison and there was no one to hear me. And if they heard me, they wouldn't have done anything. The Marines had been through this before, so they knew what to do. The two corporals grabbed me, and they were ten times a match for me, weakened by my diet and the tortures. They handled me like a child, dragging me back to the shower, each one grabbing a wrist, stretching me out between them, and then the sergeant himself went up and turned the water on.

It poured over my back and burned my raw, shaven skin. Then they turned me around and it scalded my naked chest, my belly, my cock, my balls, as it never had before. I screamed and screamed, as much from the release of my terror as from the excruciating pain.

But finally the water stopped, and I stopped, and the shower room was silent except for the drip-dripping of the shower head.

"Turn him around," the sergeant said, and the corporals rotated me, unprotesting, to face forward.

"Parade rest!" the sergeant ordered softly, and I did as I was told, realizing as I did it that I was crying, sobbing helplessly.

The two corporals stepped away from me and went down to stand on either side of the sergeant.

"Look at me!" the sergeant commanded.

I looked into his black, twinkling eyes, and I knew that he could see my defeat clearly in mine.

"Now look down," the sergeant said. "At my crotch."

I did as he said, and saw that his hand was moving slowly up and down his trouser leg. Shaken as I was, it took me a moment to realize that he was fondling an erection through the cloth. A large, clearly outlined erection. I looked away.

"Look at me!" he barked.

I tried to look at his face.

"You know where," he said, and the gentleness was gone from his deep voice.

I looked, and he stroked and stroked. I thought: It's huge! Christ, it must be huge!

"Now look at the corporal's crotch," the sergeant said, jerking his thumb left toward the redhead.

I looked, and he, too, was stroking a huge erection through the material of his trousers. Even though I looked at his crotch, I could see the red-headed corporal was smiling. And it was the smile of a schoolboy, all right! The kind of boy who is pulling the wings off butterflies.

"Now him," the sergeant said, and I duly looked over to the crotch of the second corporal. This man was olive skinned, with black hair like the sergeant's but curly instead of straight. His handsome, lean features and wide sensual mouth bore no expression at all, but his striking hazel eyes held a cruelty that made the other two seem pale. And his cock, straining through his pants, was even bigger than those of the sergeant and the redhead. Longer and thicker as well.

So this is it! I thought. This is the part where they make me suck their cocks, or else they rape me, or maybe both.

The sergeant came slowly toward me, smiling, then walked around in back of me.

"Keep looking at their cocks," he ordered.

I looked back and forth between the two huge erections. In my head I started praying, desperately. I didn't want to suck cock! I didn't want to get fucked!

I felt something on the back of my neck, something cool and hard. It touched ever so lightly, and began to move around, tickling, moving, and inching its way downward. It got right to the shaved spot above the crack of my ass and toyed with the raw skin. Then it moved over my hands. As it touched my fingers gently, I recognized it as the sergeant's night stick.

It moved down the crack of my ass, and then the sergeant began to push it in between my buttocks. He was very gentle about it, thrusting just a little harder each time, moving it back and forth so that it worked its way in toward my asshole.

Christ! I thought. He's going to fuck me with his night stick!

The club reached the sphincter and he continued to gently push and prod with it. I looked from cock to cock as the two corporals stroked themselves, and suddenly a new fear came over me. For as I looked at those two hard cocks and felt the billy club pushing its way into my ass, I began to feel the stirrings of an erection in my own cock.

Desperately I tried to blot out what was happening to me. If I got an erection, they'd think I was getting turned on by what was happening. They'd think I liked it!

The club pulled gently back from my ass and slid deftly between my legs, caressing my shaven balls with its smooth shaft and bumping gently against my cock from the underside. I felt the blood flow into my cock, and despite everything I could do, I felt my cock swell and go hard.

The red-headed corporal smiled even more broadly when he saw my hard-on. The other corporal just continued to stroke.

The sergeant withdrew the stick and walked around in front of me, looking straight into my eyes. He used the stick to stroke my cock, sliding it up one side and down the other, lifting it gently and letting it fall, stimulating it to its fullest hardness. He leaned forward, his face very close to mine, and I thought for a moment he was going to kiss me. But instead he whispered a single word, and said it with all the loathing and contempt that only a Marine sergeant can muster.

"Faggot!"

Despite everything else they had done to me, at that moment that word was much worse. I felt my face redden as the heat of a blush poured up through me. I was humiliated beyond endurance.

Then the sergeant stepped down from the shower stall and turned to me.

"Get dressed!" he said, his voice once again the soft, sure voice that it had always been.

The two corporals snapped to attention beside him, but I could see as I put my clothes on that their erections had not gone down. I finished lacing my boots and fell in between them and we marched off. At least one more day's ordeal was over!

But as we marched, I saw to my dismay that we were not going back to my cell. We were going down other corridors, deeper into the prison than I had been before. Were those erections going to get used on me today anyway?

We marched down a dimly lit hall with dust at the edges of the floors. There were steel doors on both sides, and faint sounds came from them. I thought I heard a man scream inside one; but it was muffled, and I tried to tell myself it was my imagination. We reached the end door and the sergeant opened it. I was ushered in.

The room was bare except for a hanging light bulb with a tin cover, and under it a waist-high wooden plank table about six feet long. The door shut behind me with an awful finality.

So this was where the rapes took place, I thought in terror.

Then everything changed and the terror got worse. The sergeant reached up to the wall behind the door and took down a thick, black leather razor strop. This was not the room where the rapes took place.

This was the room where the whippings took place.

Three

The sergeant walked slowly to the center of the room and laid the leather strop quietly on the table. Then he walked just as slowly back to where I was standing, and looking at me with that smile of his, loosened his collar.

The room had dark, dingy walls that must have once been painted pale green. Time had made the color uncertain, and in any event, there was not enough light to tell. Just that one bulb that hung over the table, spreading a cone of light down on the table harshly, and leaving the upper part of the room and the walls in gloom. The tin shade on the light bulb was also a cone, but a cone of darkness. It reminded me of the kind of shaded light they used to have in poolrooms.

The sergeant unbuttoned his shirt and started pulling it off.

The table was made of wooden planks, with thick, sturdy legs, braces at the bottom and under the top, and a solid plank for a top. It was about six feet long, and a little wider than a man's body. I felt my breath coming harder.

The sergeant was stripped to the waist now, and he walked over and stood next to the table, where the light fell on his chest and body but left his face in darkness. I had known that he was well built, but the uniform had covered a great deal. His chest was broad, and thickly muscled, as were his powerful arms. He had a pelt of dark, curly hair that started at his throat, spread out, and covered his chest and belly all the way down, getting thicker below his navel before it disappeared under his belt.

"Strip!" the sergeant said, "And lay face down on the table!"

The very word — strip! — was now bringing an instant response from me of fear and eagerness to obey. I began taking off my clothes, dropping them on the floor. The sergeant had hung his neatly on the peg that he'd taken the belt from.

"You'll be spending a lot of time here," the sergeant said as I peeled my teeshirt over my head. "There are a few rules you'll have to learn if you're going to get by. The first is that I don't mind your screaming, so long as I'm inflicting pain on you, and so long as we're in this room. I don't want you whimpering or begging before I start, though! I can't stand that; and if you start it, I'll make it worse for you. The second is that I don't mind you begging and pleading, so long as it's something I've approved of you pleading for. You are not ever to beg for mercy, or for me to stop, you understand?"

"Sir! Yes, Sir!" I said, dropping my dungarees and pushing down my shorts.

"The food we give you," the sergeant said, "is designed to keep you cleaned out. There's a medical reason for that. If you have anything much in your guts when I'm whipping you, it might cause real injury. I have no intention of injuring you, only hurting you."

I walked naked across the room and climbed on the table, lying face down.

"From now on," the sergeant said, "we won't do much talking. Training you with the basics doesn't require much talk."

The two corporals came across the room, their boots booming on the wooden floor. They stood by the head of the table, at my sides, and pinned me, each one putting one hand on my shoulder, just in the middle of the shoulder blade, and one hand on my arm, just above the elbow. They pushed down forcefully, so that it hurt. In this position the upper half of my body couldn't move at all. My arms hung over the sides of the table, and I figured the best thing to do would be to grip the sides of the table against the pain.

It was a long time coming, but I knew that was so I could anticipate it. I became intensely aware of the feeling of my naked, shaven body against the smooth, cool wood of the table top. My chest, my belly, my shaven cock scrunched up under me against my belly, my smooth shaven balls hanging down between my legs and touching the wood.

Then I heard the whir of the strap and the first blow landed hard across my ass.

I didn't cry out, or even grunt; I just took the stinging pain of it. It was only the first, after all. There was no sense giving the sergeant everything he wanted right at the beginning. There was a long time more, then the second blow fell, harder, across my ass.

"I'm giving you the count of ten between lashes," the sergeant whispered. "To let the pain develop."

The third blow landed, *thwack*, across my back. Above the middle, but below where the corporals held me. I had been prepared for another blow across my ass, but this one caught me unaware, and I grunted with surprise as much as pain.

Whack, across my ass again, now burning with the accumulated pain of three lashes. And I found myself counting, slowly, One, Two, Three, Four, Five, Six, Seven, Eight, Nine . . .

Ten.

Whack!

On my back again, up high, between the shoulder blades where they had me pinned.

I realized suddenly that the reason he'd told me how much the count was between lashes would be to make me think it out, to let me build up anticipation of the coming blow. Two extra touches to make it worse, the slow welling of the pain and the anguish of anticipation!

Whack!

On my back again, but lower, where the belt hadn't hit before.

Whack!

Across my ass again at a new angle.

Whack! across my ass, two, three, four, five . . .

Ten, *Whack!* on my back two, three . . .

And *Whack!* And *Whack!* And *Whack!* And *Whack!*

I don't know how long he beat me, or how many strokes of the black leather razor strop he landed, but finally it was over and the two corporals released my shoulders.

"Get up and get dressed!" the sergeant ordered, and I heard him walking back to where he had hung his clothes.

I climbed up from the table, my back and ass screaming with the pain, and started to dress. I didn't know whether I had done any screaming for the sergeant or not. My mind was numb, everything in the world was blotted out by the one reality of the agony of my body.

They marched me back to my cell and I sank down on my cot, face down, and cried myself to sleep.

The next day there was a change in my routine and I figured out at once the reason for it.

When I finished the shower, the sergeant ordered me about face, parade rest, and started the scalding water on my front. After I was sufficiently burned on the balls and cock, he ordered the about face, parade rest with my back to the shower, so that the burning I got on my back would be fresher for the blows to come.

He didn't do the bit with the corporals fingering their cocks, or him playing with my ass with his billy club; he just had me dress and marched me straight to the room with the wooden table. Then it was: "Strip! And lie face down on the table." — And the corporals pinned my shoulders, and then the belt was whirring through the air, and *Whack!* The strop landed across my back and I screamed.

The scalding water, and the whipping of the day before, had done a good job of tenderizing me and making the pain more intense.

As the blows fell, one after another, always with that slow count of ten between them, my mind tried to find a way out of the pain and the panic. As my ass and then my back took lash after lash, I found myself struggling helplessly against the force of the corporals' hands on my shoulders and arms. I found to my dismay that I was trying to count the lashes, to think about anything but the awful pain.

. . . Eight, nine, ten, *Whack!*

Was that ten lashes?

. . . Eight, nine, ten, *Whack!* across my ass.

Eleven?

I wasn't so much struggling as squirming, and I knew that it didn't make any difference and that, if anything, seeing my naked ass squirming as the black leather strop came down on it probably pleased the sergeant more than if I'd held still.

I tried not to scream, but it wasn't any good. The pain was just too awful. And then it was over.

"Get dressed!" the sergeant ordered quietly, and he got dressed, and I got dressed, and they marched me back to my cell.

As I lay face down on my cot crying and moaning, I realized that he hadn't said anything at all to me the whole time, except to give me direct orders. A new fear rose up in me. He'd said the day before that I would spend a lot of time in the room with the wooden table.

I realized that something of what had been holding me together (as much as I had held) was the fact that each new day brought new horrors. Though that thought was the first step to fear, it was also the prospect that things would change; probably for the worse, but they would change, and that was something, however bleak, to look forward to. Suppose things stopped changing? Suppose this were it? Suppose every day from now on was going to be just like this one?

The next day seemed to bear out the worst of my fears. They came and got me; I showered, they scalded my balls and then my incredibly tender ass and back; and then they took me to the room with the wooden table.

"Strip! And lay face down on the table!" the sergeant said, and then the whipping began.

But something new was added, and something happened inside me, and it was worse than I could have feared. On the previous day my insane and agonized mind had counted something like twenty strokes of the strop, give or take a few missed in agony. Now twenty came and went, and still the whipping went on!

Twenty-three lashes.

Whack!

Twenty-four lashes.

Whack!

I began screaming in earnest now, not merely at each lash, but constantly as the blows rained down.

Whack!

Thirty-five.

Whack!

Thirty-six.

Whack!

Eight, nine, ten. . .

Thirty-nine!

That part of my mind that counted the lashes continued to do so long after the pain prevented me from really thinking. But another part of my mind became aware that as the pain reached a stage beyond which my body could not tolerate it, my balls drew up slowly and my cock got harder and harder. When the whipping stopped; there were only two things in my mind: I had taken sixty lashes, and my cock was hard as a rock!

"Get up and get dressed!" the sergeant said, but I didn't move. I still don't know whether it was because I couldn't move with so much pain or because I dared not move for fear they would see my erection.

Abruptly the two corporals pulled me up and yanked me to my feet.

"Parade rest!" the sergeant barked, and even moving that much was torture as I fell into the posture, obeying, confused, my hard cock sticking up in front of my shaven belly.

The sergeant walked over, his bare, hairy chest dripping with sweat. He wiped his forehead with his hairy forearm and hung the black razor strop around his neck. Then he folded his arms across his chest, spread his legs apart just like my parade rest stance, and smiled broadly, his even white teeth gleaming in the dimness.

"Look at that, boys!" the sergeant said. "Quite a nice, hard dork for a faggot!"

There was so much Marine contempt in his voice that if I'd been capable of feeling anything, I would have crumbled. But I was beyond blushing. All the blood that could reach the surface of my skin was suffused through the agony of my back and my ass. I was beyond any kind of humiliation. The two corporals, who had been standing at formal attention, relaxed their posture now and began to laugh at me quietly.

The sergeant reached out with his billy club and gave my hard cock a playful bat. It sprang back to attention with even greater rigidity.

"Get dressed!" the sergeant said.

They let me take a long time to dress, and the march back to my cell was slow. When the door closed behind me, I stood still for a long time, unable to walk because of the pain and shaking with such an amount of fear that everything else was blotted out.

At least I was able to get to my bed, take off the clothes that now were as painful as a coating of napalm, and lie face down in the hope of sleep.

But I couldn't sleep. I hurt too much and I was too afraid. I knew that if I slept I would be awakened to another nightmare day. Finally, long, long after they had delivered me, my breakfast was slid under the door, and my mind and body, both exhausted, were shocked by the tin dishes rattling, and I went over the edge, into unconsciousness.

Breakfast, lunch, and dinner were all lined up cold on their trays on the floor when I finally awoke. I had been able after the first two whippings to throw off most of the pain during my sleep. But now my body cried out with the previous day's abuse. Not just the pain at the surface level, but pain right down into the muscles. I felt as if I had swum a thousand miles. Every muscle ached, and my skin was on fire.

My reason told me it would be better to die, right then and there. But a man's reason is poor competitor for his instinct for survival. I ate the dinner; and after a while the food gave me strength, and I had cold, tasteless lunch as well.

By that time I had figured out that something different was happening. I had been through a whole day without my session in the room with the wooden table. Without any trace of the Marines!

Or had I? I asked myself. With the unchanging light in my cell I had no way to measure time. They could have opened that little port in the door, seen me passed out, and slid in two extra trays just to make me think I had had a day off! To disorient me even further!

It occurred to me to try and figure out how long I had been in the prison.

My first day was obviously the one on which I'd been incarcerated. That much, at least, was certain. If they had really taken me for one 'session' each day, then the second day was the time they had begun scalding me, just my back. The third day was the one when he'd whirled me around with an about face and I'd been doubled over with the pain. That made the fourth day the one when he had me shaved. The fifth day was the one when I'd broken, and offered to sign away my discharge; the one when the sergeant had told me there was no hope, that I would have to stick out the eight weeks. That was also the day when the sergeant had begun to play with me sexually, to humiliate me and call me 'faggot.' And it was the day when the whippings began.

The sixth day was the day the sergeant had reversed the order of my scalding, so that my back would be at its tenderest. That made the day he'd increased the number of lashes, the day when I got an erection from the whipping, the seventh! And that had only been yesterday!

I had only been in the Brig a week! I still had seven weeks to go!

I sat and cried for a while in fear, then it hit me that once again I was being manipulated. Whether a whole day had passed or not, this time alone was another kind of 'session.' The sergeant was giving me space to recover and, incidentally, time to think about the enormous span of weeks ahead. Time to build up more apprehension, more fear.

I puked everything I'd eaten.

They tell me fear can do that to you. So can desire if it builds too long without release. It has something to do with the way your body shoots juices into your digestive system when you're under stress. If you have a way to get rid of the adrenaline, fine; but if you don't, you end up puking.

After I puked I felt better. The physical part of the fear was relieved, even if the mental fear and the physical pain wasn't. I waited until my stomach was growling like a lion, then I ate the least appetizing of the three meals, the stale breakfast.

I knew that if I let my muscles tighten up, things would be worse when they whipped me again; so I put the food trays together in a stack, jumbling all the tin dishes on top, and stowed them in the corner. Then I did calisthenics, exercising through the pain until I finally got some sense that it was easing up a little. After that I was tired, so I lay down and went to sleep. Thus ended my eighth day.

My body, I discovered, was a better clock than the various appearances of food and my captors. Even though I hadn't eaten my three meals (or, rather, retained them), I was up with the trots at the right time, and shortly thereafter the Marines came for me. I noted that my dishes were still sitting in the corner and noted idly that my cell was cleaned and my dishes picked up each day while I was at my session.

They marched me into the shower. I stripped, tossed my very stale clothes into the hamper, showered, and then, to my surprise, the sergeant didn't have them start the water. I stood facing that ominous shower head for what seemed like an eternity; then the two corporals came up into the shower stall and stood on each side of it. They started playing with themselves, and their big cocks got hard, stretching the fabric of their pants tight and showing the outline of the shaft and head quite clearly.

I felt the sergeant's night stick on the back of my neck again, and I shivered. Goosebumps broke out all over my body as it moved slowly down my back, over my hands, and in between the cheeks of my ass. I felt it push and prod, back and forth, working its way in at my asshole. Then it withdrew a little and slid between my legs.

As my cock got hard, it didn't surprise me at all. I knew now that the sergeant was able to manipulate my physical responses in ways that I didn't fully understand. But I felt fairly secure about it, because it was, after all, somebody else manipulating me; it wasn't something that was a natural part of me. I was sure that I would never have gotten hard from a man handling me if I hadn't been broken down and conditioned to do whatever the sergeant wanted. When I got out, everything would be all right. I'd find my girlfriend, and maybe the engagement would be more than a 'maybe.'

The billy club drew back, and once more it sought out my asshole. It pushed and prodded some more.

"I can tell you like that, faggot," the sergeant whispered right at my ear. "I can tell it feels real good to you. And I'm not surprised. That's how I want you to feel. And how I want you to feel is just the way you are going to feel, I promise you. You've heard about how the commies brainwash captives to make them believe what they want? Well, Yankee ingenuity is way ahead of that old stuff. Uncle Sam doesn't care what you believe, so long as you do what you're told. What's on your mind doesn't matter, so long as you jump when Uncle says jump. That's why they let you sailor boys do all the talking about pacifism and all the rest of that shit. It doesn't matter what you think or say, so long as you jump when the order comes. But you stopped jumping, sailor boy, and that means we didn't train you well enough. So now we're training you some more. When we're finished with you, you'll be as well-trained as the very best kind of dog. You'll speak on command, and you'll sit, and you'll sit up, and you'll heel, and you'll roll over, and you'll beg. You'll be very good at begging, in particular. You'll keep on thinking whatever you want, but you'll do whatever I say. That's the part that will scare you the most in the end. You'll be able to think for yourself, but you'll only be able to act on what I say. I will control your feelings, and when I want you to cringe, you will cringe. But better still, when I want you turned on, you'll get turned on. And it won't be by girls or any of the normal things. I'm going to train you to be turned on by pain and humiliation. I'm going to fix you so that the only thing that gets that cock of yours hard is a tough man standing over you."

I felt the sergeant lay his hand on my leg, then move it slowly up and play with my balls, then slide it around my cock and slowly begin to masturbate me. His voice was so low and so soothing that I could barely hear it. He made his words sound like endearments, for all that what he said was definitely not love-making.

"You can feel it happening already," he whispered. "You felt it at your last whipping, and you'll feel it again and again. It's only natural that it should be that way. Your body and the deep, deep levels of your mind have to find a way to escape from the pain. And the only way they can escape is through the door of pleasure. When the stimulation is so intense that you can't find a way out, your body turns the pain into pleasure and you start getting hot. Soon you'll start taking that escape route sooner and sooner. The first lash will make your cock go hard as rock. The very sound of a belt slapping will make you helpless with lust, and you'll want more. When I'm finished with you, you'll be begging for the belt and anything else I want. You'll be the best-trained dog I ever had. And you'll be as queer as a three-dollar bill."

The feeling of the club against my asshole, the strong, ever-faster stroking of his hand on my cock made everything he said seem all right. I didn't care what he was saying, because I felt my balls tightening and the fiery explosion of an orgasm building up down inside. I knew that at any moment I was going to come and that anything he was saying was all right so long as I shot my load under his strong, steady stroking.

As I felt the orgasm starting, he let go. He pulled the stick away from my ass, and I started to moan. My eyes were closed, and I realized that his hypnotic voice had stopped.

And at that same exact second when my mind hit on that word hypnotic! — And I realized that he was not only using my body, but reaching into my mind with hypnosis: the scalding water hit!

I screamed.

If it had been a second later, the orgasm would have come. And then I knew what he said about the pain into pleasure would have taken over and the water wouldn't have hurt; it would have been part of a sexual explosion. But the sergeant was a master of manipulating other men's bodies, and he knew precisely when to strike.

My hard cock at its most sensitive was hit by the full force of the scalding water. As I screamed, it shriveled; and my balls drew up inside me. The pleasure I had been feeling at anticipation of the orgasm was turned into ultimate agony. The sergeant had pushed me backwards through those gates!

I barely heard his "About face!" but my body responded anyway, just as he said it would; and my raw back was scalded by the sudden agony, just the way my front had been the first time. I started to faint and fall over, but the sergeant knew what reaction to look for. He stopped the water and the two corporals held me up and he broke a vial of ammonia under my nose, yanking me back to consciousness of my pain.

"Get dressed!" he barked.

They marched me down to the room with the wooden table and I stripped and lay face down on it. The two corporals held my shoulders and arms and I felt the lash of the first stroke on my ass.

Then the second, then the third, and then the fourth landed on my back.

But even as the sergeant had predicted, even by the time the fifth and sixth strokes were landing and searing into my back, my cock was rising to hardness, turning pain into arousal.

When the tenth stroke had landed across my ass, the whipping stopped and I felt the sergeant's hand on the back of my neck. It moved gently, just as the billy club had before, down my back, toying with the shaved spot above my ass, over the globes of my ass, and then down the crack of my ass to my hole. I felt his finger prod gently, then, just as gently, start to push in. He only pushed it in a little way; but it was a relief from the pain of the whipping, and my body responded. I felt my ass contract as if to draw the finger further in and my prick stiffen more between my belly and the table top.

The sergeant gently withdrew the finger, then the strop whirred again and I felt it land against my ass.

Eight, nine, ten strokes, and then the whipping once again paused. His right hand on the back of my neck moved down, his finger pushing into my asshole, this time a little deeper. This time when he felt the contractions he pulled it slowly out and moved it down between my legs, taking my shaven balls into his hand and massaging them gently, encircling them with his fingers, tugging them gently downward, and finally laying them on the cool wood.

Then the whipping again, ten more agonizing strokes.

This time his finger plunged deep into my asshole and he began to move it around. I had never guessed that having something up my ass could give me pleasure; I would never have believed it. But he knew just what to do to me to make it unbearably exciting. He massaged my prostate through the intestinal wall, not the rough way a doctor checks it out, but with skill, making me moan with pleasure. Then he withdrew and worked on my balls some more.

Finally he put one arm under my belly and lifted me up a little, and with the other hand he grasped my swollen cock. He squeezed it, slid the skin back and forth, then pulled it downward, aiming straight toward my feet, and lowered me back to the table.

Now the pressure of my cock against the wood made me force my ass up into the air. The sergeant slid his finger in again and I groaned with excitement.

"Looks just like a cat in heat," he said softly and contemptuously. "Just waiting for some big tom to shove his prick right up it!"

Then he slid the finger out and I heard the razor strop whir; and I knew even before it struck that it would land on my ass, so helplessly and invitingly turned up for him. I writhed and squirmed as the blows landed, pinned at the shoulders by the corporals and forced by my own cock to hold my ass up to the blows!

He had paused to stimulate me during the first thirty lashes. He went right through the second thirty with only those awful counts of ten between them. I felt the corporals release my shoulders and the sergeant told me to get up.

I turned on my side to let my cock spring back upright. As I lay for a second gasping and sweating, I saw the two corporals were leaving the room.

So, I thought, the sergeant has been getting my ass ready for his cock, and this was going to be it!

I got up off the table, and would have leaned my ass against it for a moment to steady myself if it hadn't hurt so much.

"Parade rest!" the sergeant ordered.

I did it, and the sergeant came around the table. He stood in front of me and slowly hung the black leather strop around his neck. He was sweating, and droplets of moisture trickled down all over his chest through the thick mat of dark, curly hair. He stepped forward up close to me and the strong, clean smell of his sweat overpowered me. He reached out both hands and began to play with my tits, pulling at them, massaging them, tweaking them. They quickly grew hard and stood out.

The sergeant took his billy club and, holding onto both ends, rolled it up and down the front of his pants. I could see that he had a hard-on, and I figured I knew what he meant to do with it. Then, to my complete astonishment, he sank down and put his knees on my bare feet, kneeling before me.

With his left hand he took the billy club and slid it up against my asshole, not pushing it in but almost. With his right hand he grasped my balls and began to tug at them, slowly, rhythmically, as he moved the club in and out.

Then he opened his mouth and took the head of my swollen cock into it and began to lick and suck at the head.

I nearly came apart at the combination of pain and pleasure, but I held my hands firmly behind me, afraid that if I moved it might all end, and equally afraid that this was just another build-up for another torture.

He took my cock deeper into his mouth, and the rhythm of the club at my ass and his tugging my balls increased. His head moved back and forth as he sucked my cock deeper and deeper into his mouth, each stroke going a little further in, each licking of the underside of the head going a little faster.

I felt my arms and legs stiffening. I felt my ass tighten. I knew what was about to come.

The sergeant took his mouth off of my cock, but he kept up the stimulation of my balls and my ass.

"You want to come?" he whispered.

"Oh, yeah!" I moaned.

"That's not the way you say it," he said softly, amused.

"Sir! Yes, Sir! I want to come, Sir!" I rapped out.

"You can only come if I let you," the sergeant whispered. "Let me hear you beg for it!"

"Sir! Yes, Sir! Please, Sir, let me come, Sir!"

"Then I was right all along, wasn't I?" he asked.

"Sir! Yes, Sir!" I agreed, not caring what he meant.

"You're nothing but a shit-faced little faggot, are you?"

"Sir! Yes, Sir!"

"Let me hear you say it," he said.

"Sir! Yes, Sir! I'm nothing but a shit-faced little faggot, Sir!"

"You're just another queer sailor!"

"Sir! Yes, Sir! I'm just another queer sailor, Sir!"

"Tell me you're a queer!"

"Sir! Yes, Sir! I'm a queer, Sir!"

"Tell me you're a queer!"

"Sir! Yes, Sir! I'm a queer, Sir!"

"Tell me you're a queer!"

"Sir! Yes, Sir! I'm a queer, Sir!"

"Tell me you're a queer!"

"Sir! Yes, Sir! I'm a queer, Sir!"

He plunged my cock all the way into his mouth, yanked down on my balls, and shoved the stick hard up against my ass. I felt the come boiling up from inside me, shooting through my cock. Then it exploded out the head and shot into his hot, sucking mouth, wave after wave of white hot lava, shooting all the pain from me back to the sergeant who'd caused it.

Four

I woke the next morning with the feeling that everything was ninety degrees from true. My back and ass ached like fury, and from the tears that had dried on my face I knew I had once again cried myself to sleep. I knew that what had happened to me the day before was real, but I felt oddly at peace about it.

Had the sergeant forced a true admission from me? Was I a queer? I had certainly gotten off on what he did to me.

But it all seemed backwards. If I was queer, then I should have been sucking cock, shouldn't I? And how did it square that he was sucking me off, yet he was *not* queer?

I emptied my bowels, the door opened, and they marched me off to the showers.

Once again I was scalded, once again my body was played with until I got an erection. It didn't take long either, for my mind went right where the sergeant wanted it to go, to the blow job he'd given me the day before.

I was marched to the room with the wooden table, the door shut behind us, and the next variation was set forth.

It was not the sergeant who took down the black leather razor strop this time, it was the red-headed corporal with the freckles and the eyes that pulled wings off butterflies.

He walked over to the table slowly, languidly, and dropped the belt onto it. He had that boyish grin on his face, like a kid on the way to the circus, and I knew that whatever was going to happen to me, he was going to enjoy it. He sauntered slowly back to the hook on the wall and began to peel off his tie and shirt. He didn't fix me with his eye the way the sergeant always did. He looked up and down my body as if looking at it for the first time, sizing me up, almost the way a wrestler sizes an opponent. More, the way men look a woman up and down when they want to be particularly insulting!

His chest was smooth and the freckles spread out over it, drawing attention to his hard pink nipples and the youthful pinkness of his skin. I could imagine him burning to death in strong sunlight if he ever went out to the beach. His shoulders were broad, the bones showing, but every muscle on his body was delineated. He wasn't beefy like the sergeant. He was lean, tough, corded. His arms were like pistons wrapped in thick ropes or cables.

He sauntered back over to the table, picked up the strop, doubled it, and made it snap. I felt a shiver run over me.

"Strip!" he ordered, still languidly, and with a trace of drawl. "And lay face down on the table!"

I did as I was told; and for the first time I felt the pressure of the sergeant's hands as he and the dark corporal pinned my shoulders and arms. Then the strop whirred and I felt the first blow land flat across the middle of my back.

Somehow I didn't feel the urge to cry out for a long while. At least it seemed a long while, for I noticed the corporal counted far more slowly than the sergeant. I didn't know whether the longer time between lashes gave my body time to recover or the pain to develop more fully. Even lying there being whipped, I was still in possession of that confusion in which I'd waked.

The ten lashes were finished and I felt the corporal's hand on the back of my neck. But the corporal didn't move gently downward the way the sergeant had. He kneaded, he pushed, he pinched lightly, like a masseur. My skin being raw, it hurt, and I felt myself squirm. He liked that, so he worked a little harder, down my back, around the globes of my ass, then into my asshole.

He wasn't tender about that, either. No little prodding and pushing, just a steady movement that took his finger all the way in. I grunted, and he played around in there, and my erection came on, just the way I knew it would. His finger pulled out, abruptly, and the belt came down again.

After the second ten strokes the finger fucking got a little rougher, and when he played with my balls, he yanked and squeezed. He wasn't nearly as much concerned with turning me on as he was with hurting me; but it was obvious that the pattern was something the sergeant had determined, and it was going to be carried out. After the third set of ten I yelled when he shoved his finger up me, and again when he crushed my balls in his fist. But the way he just reached under me, grabbed my cock, and yanked it around and downward was the worst. I found myself struggling, trying to get my prick to some bearable position, even as the first stroke fell against my newly-upturned ass.

The second thirty strokes fell faster than the first thirty, and with increasing rapidity. I could tell that he was getting excited by what he was doing. Then it was over and I was standing there, the sergeant and the dark corporal gone, and this all-American boy panting and smiling at me, the sweat trickling down his chest in little clear droplets.

He hung the belt around his neck and without preamble reached out and took hold of my tits. He grabbed each one with a thumb and forefinger, pinched hard, then twisted them as hard as he could. It was so sudden I reacted without thinking. I groaned and my hands came up and took hold of his wrists.

"Put 'em back!" he snarled, his eyes blazing with pleasure, and he twisted harder.

Despite the pain I did as I was told, resuming parade rest, but unable to hold my body straight as he tortured me. After a moment he let go, stepped back, and laughed.

"I just love queers," he said. "But some of 'em just don't know how to behave!"

He slapped me hard across the face. Then he went down on his knees, resting them on my feet, and shoved his billy club up against my asshole. He pushed it so hard that I thought I would have to go up on tip-toe, except he was kneeling on my toes. Maybe, I figured, he wanted me to slide onto it. But the slap had cleared my head, and I wasn't about to cooperate with him.

He grabbed my balls, crushing them for a moment, then encircling them with his thumb and forefinger near the base and pulling downward. I was torn now between the stick at my ass shoving me upward and the hand around my balls pulling me downward. Then he took my cock in his mouth and started sucking.

He was no more gentle about the way he sucked cock than he was about the way he handled my balls. He sucked hard and fast and furious, drawing me all the way into his throat, sliding all the way back so that the head nearly fell out of his mouth. Then he'd suck hard and the whole length would be pulled in again. And when just the head was in his mouth he'd run his rough tongue all over it, scraping it, making me want to scream with pleasure that was almost in itself pain.

He took my cock down his throat and suddenly he bit down hard. I twisted, fighting to hold my position and not grab for his head. He drew my cock slowly out, biting hard each quarter of an inch along the shaft. Then he sucked harder and faster. I wouldn't have thought it was possible, but he kept sucking faster. And I felt the orgasm coming on. I couldn't contain myself. I moaned.

He pulled his mouth off and yanked hard on my balls; and I felt the club push so hard that it actually forced its way a little into my rectum.

"Come on, faggot boy, you know what to say!"

"Sir! Yes, Sir! I'm a shit-faced faggot sailor boy, Sir! I'm nothing but a queer, Sir! Please, Sir, let me come, Sir!"

"Come on!" he said, squeezing and shoving harder. "The sarge wants you to say it over and over!"

"I'm queer, Sir! I'm queer, Sir! I'm queer, Sir!"

And I just kept saying it over and over, seeing but not looking at his happy, malicious face, with its creamy complexion and its freckles and its blue eyes and red hair, and feeling him crush my balls and push into my ass.

Finally he seemed satisfied that I was saying it right and he went to work on my prick again, and then I came. What felt like buckets of come shot up through my cock, raging through the head as he sucked and tongued and bit on it. I felt like I was going to choke him with it, but he kept on sucking! There wasn't any more in me, but the bastard kept on sucking; and finally my hands went out from behind me and seized him by the hair, trying to pull his hot mouth off me.

The minute I touched his head, he pulled back, and in one motion he was on his feet. The club dangled from his belt, and the razor strop was whirring through the air to land with a brutal lash full across my chest.

"When I say stand, I mean stand!" he snarled, and the strop landed across my chest from the other direction. "Now, get dressed, you stinking queer!"

I expected it when the next day it was the dark corporal's turn to whip me.

As usual, the sergeant conducted the preliminaries at the shower, then I was marched to the whipping room. The door was closed and the dark corporal took charge, quietly and efficiently stripping to the waist without so much as glancing at me.

I did, however, look at him. His chest was smooth, except for some dark, long strands of hair around his large, dark brown nipples. His build was not bulkier than the sergeant's, nor was it harder than the redhead's; but it was far more perfect than either. He had the washboard stomach that most men don't even try for. He had the perfectly-rounded curves of muscle under the skin that leave no capability in doubt, but which do not seem over-done. His skin was a dark, almost golden tan, as if he had Amerind blood in slight degree. Some Chicanos have that golden color when they are young; most don't. I didn't know what to expect at his hands. He had only ever shown the slightest amusement at what we were doing, even though he had shown the largest and thickest erection. His hazel eyes were a mystery and one that held a great deal of fear for me.

When he finally said: "Strip! And lay face down on the table," I was startled. From the sergeant it had been suave and commanding. From the redhead it had been bullying and cruel. From this man it was level and business-like as if he had asked me to pass the butter. I almost expected him to add: "Please."

I got up on the table, feeling the cool wood under my shaved body, and wondering what special variations the dark corporal would make in my ordeal. Then as the first blow fell across my ass, I knew!

In all the whippings, in all the agony I had endured, the sergeant, and then the redhead, had been holding back. They had not been whipping me with as much force as they could have. That was how I had endured sixty lashes a day for three days! Now, the dark corporal was not holding back. I screamed at the first blow, at least twice as hard as anything the others had delivered, and I kept on screaming, my mind numbed by both fear and panic.

And it didn't matter that I got an erection all the same. It didn't matter when the first ten blows had landed and I felt the dark corporal's business-like hand moving smoothly down toward my anal sphincter. I knew I couldn't live through any more. I knew I had to die from the sheer pain. I willed myself to die. I willed my body to go into shock.

But the corporal's business-like finger moved into my ass and moved around, prodding, pushing, and then I felt a second finger slide in next to it. The two fingers revolved, stretching the sphincter muscle, and then a third slid in. I would have tightened in fear if I hadn't been too afraid to feel any more. The pain of the body was so bad that all I could feel about my asshole was relief that I wasn't being whipped.

But the respite didn't last, and the second ten lashes fell as hard as the first. I kept on screaming this time, even as his fingers slowly stretched my asshole wider. Then I felt a new sensation. Something cool and hard was sliding into my asshole. I realized it was a billy club slipping in, deeper and deeper. Was this what it was like being fucked?

With the club deep inside me I felt him grope for my balls, pull them steadily downward, then start squeezing. I had thought the pain of his whipping me was the worst thing a man could feel, but I was wrong. The agony a man feels when his balls are twisted and crushed is worse than anything that can be done to the rest of his body. And the dark corporal knew just how to crush and twist my balls to cause the maximum of pain!

By the time he let go and slid the club out of my ass I was almost longing for the whipping. But the first lash changed that. I felt I would lose my voice if I screamed much more, and then what would I do? Would the pain that I was throwing out with my shrieking build up inside till I exploded?

He stopped. He shoved his finger up my ass, then another, then a third, then all four of his fingers. Was he going to try and shove his whole fist up there, I wondered? But no, then came the club sliding sensuously in, and then the agony of my balls being tortured that I realized served at least to distract me from my whipping.

Finally he pulled my cock down, and my ass shoved up in the air as I kept on screaming, unable to express anything more, unable to face the terrible reality of the coming thirty lashes.

When the whipping was finally over I must have lost consciousness. I don't remember anything but the ultimate, unfocused pain, and then the acrid smell of ammonia under my nose as I lay on the wooden table, sweating, trembling, shaking with chills.

I was alone in the room with the dark corporal, and I began to cry, laying there, wondering what he would do to me. He tossed the broken ammonia vial into the corner, then walked over and leaned against the wall.

I couldn't take my eyes off him. He had been whipping me with twice the force the other men had used, yet his chest barely glistened from the effort. They had shown different kinds of tension, yet he seemed completely at ease. His eyes showed me that I meant nothing to him. I was a job, like cleaning a latrine. I was something he'd been told to do, and he would do it. And do it well. But he had no emotional involvement in it.

After a while he gestured with his head that I was to get up. I did so, and stood at parade rest, knowing that was what was expected of me. He let me stand that way a while, wondering; then he bent down and took off his boots.

They were the usual boots that Marine MPs wore, and had long laces. He took one of the laces carefully out of the boot, then threaded it through the top two holes as if he were going to relace them upside down.

"Stand a little more away from the table," he said.

I stepped forward.

He came over in front of me and knelt down. He balanced the boot on his knee, then wound the long laces around my scrotum, making them into a tube that stretched my balls further and further downward. Finally he tied the ends of the laces into a neat bow and lowered the boot, so that it hung from my balls, the top just level with my knees, the heel almost touching the floor. He pulled the boot way out in front of me and let it go, swinging back and forth between my legs, pulling hard on my balls with each swing.

"Keep that swinging," he said. "If you let it stop, I'll make you sorry."

He stood there a moment watching. The boot started to slow. I rocked my pelvis back and forth, as if I were fucking, and the boot picked up momentum. He nodded.

Next he reached into his pants pocket and pulled out a pair of abnormally shaped alligator clips. He reached out and tweaked my nipples a couple of times each, exciting them to stiffness; then he put the clips on them. The tiny teeth bit in like fury, and I bit my lip against the pain. I wasn't really thinking by that point, only reacting. If there were any part of me that was not in pain, he would find it soon and put it in pain!

From the leather pouch at his side he took out a slim white plastic tube that narrowed at one end, then flared out. Recessed in the flared part was a slide-switch. He moved around in back of me and I felt the smooth tip of the plastic device against my asshole. He pushed slowly and steadily, and I felt it slide in all the way, stopping only when my sphincter closed around the narrow part. Then he must have pushed the button, because a deep vibrating started inside my ass, and my cock, only partly hard, stiffened all the way.

He stood beside me and watched me, gauging me. After a while he took the leather belt from around his own waist and, looping it through the buckle, put it around my neck like a dog collar. I felt it tighten like a noose around my neck.

Holding the collar tight, he reached down and began to play with my hard cock. He didn't do anything fancy, he just held it in his grip and moved the skin back and forth. Each stroke was a deep, complete one, and his grip was firm. It occurred to me that if he continued like that he could keep me at a peak all night, but I didn't dare say anything. I didn't know whether he wanted me to or not.

When he had me helpless and moaning, he spoke quietly.

"Got anything you want to say?"

I blurted out all the stuff the sergeant had taught me to say, as if it were my Sunday school catechism. I told him over and over that I was queer.

But still he didn't change his rhythm, still he held me by the collar, still I was obliged to keep that boot swinging and endure the clips on my tits and writhe with the pleasure of the vibrator up my ass and his hand on my cock. Finally my words died out and I blurted: "Sir! Please, Sir! Tell me what you want me to do, Sir!" I found I was crying, not from the pain, but from sheer desire.

"I want you to beg me to kiss you," he said matter-of-factly.

"Sir! Please, Sir! Please kiss me, Sir!" I begged.

He yanked on the collar so that my head pulled sideways, then his mouth was on mine. His tongue plunged into my mouth, thrusting, ravenous, more like a raging cock than a tongue. His lips covered mine, and his teeth pushed between mine, forcing them apart as his hungry tongue sought to climb further down my throat. I felt my lips cut against my teeth and I tasted blood. I felt as if my jaws would be pried apart by the savage force of what he was doing. I had never imagined a kiss could be anything so brutal, even from a man. The collar choked me; his tongue threatened to cut off my air. I found my survival mechanism going into gear, and I felt myself go off balance as I started to struggle with him.

But he owned my body at that moment. My hands were free and my legs, but my cock and balls were his as were my tits and ass. He had me by the throat, and he was in my mouth, even as I started to struggle, he did something to my cock that I couldn't understand; but that got the reaction he wanted. Helpless, struggling, I came, shooting out past his hand white droplets flinging themselves into the air and scattering on the floor. His hand moved on my cock, his tongue plunged into my mouth, and the world seemed to dissolve for me until it was all over.

Then he took the vibrator out of my ass, the clips off my tits, the boot off my balls, and said: "Lick it up. I don't want the floor in this place left a mess by the likes of you."

And so it was that the first come I ever tasted was not that of my Marine guardians, but my own, licked up off the dirty wooden floor of the room with the wooden table.

Five

After the dark corporal whipped me, they let me rest for three days. I knew it was three days because of the dishes and the partially eaten food that piled up in the corner of my cell.

I don't remember the first day at all. I think I slept through it, that being the only way my body and mind could cope with the pain. It's a funny thing about pain, but it's always worst right *now!* The fact that you were whipped yesterday doesn't matter when you are lying on your cot face down and feeling the welts tear you apart.

The second day I was taken to the medical officers by some strange Marines and checked over. I suppose they wanted to make sure there was no permanent damage, and I'm sure there wasn't. The sergeant would never allow that. When they released me at the end of eight weeks, I knew there would not be any trace that I could show to the press. But whether there would be any spirit left in me to go to the press, I doubted!

By the third day I was thinking again, but I was still groggy, like a man with a hangover. I knew what was coming was going to be worse, but I couldn't imagine how. If they let the dark corporal whip me again I knew there would be damage. I had caught sight of my back and ass in a mirror in the clinic, and there were welts this time, and bruises. Much more damage and the skin would break, and then there would be scars.

The fourth morning I got up and shit as usual. Whatever else happened, my body was on schedule! I waited, wondering how long it would be this time. I could feel the welts on my back with my finger tips, and I could see those on my ass. But the pain had subsided a lot, and I figured they knew that.

Sure enough, the door opened at the usual time. The fear wasn't so bad, having had three days to build, but also three to contemplate the fact that I was going to live, no matter what.

It was the dark corporal. He stepped inside and closed the door behind him. Instantly my heart started racing. Was he going to beat me again? Was that all, from now on, I would get?

He stood there, idly, as if waiting for someone on a street corner. His hazel eyes moved casually around the room, taking in the details of the dirty dishes, the rumpled bed. It took him a long time to get to me. I was sitting on the edge of the bed, paralyzed.

He glanced at me and I felt a chill, but he didn't bother to look at me for long. He went back to examining the room, as if the seatless toilet was more interesting than I was. Finally I figured that he was waiting for me to do something, so I stood and came to attention.

Still he waited, and after a while I figured that what I had done was not what he wanted. More, that I was going to have to figure it out for myself. I tried parade rest, the posture that all three of the Marines seemed to favor. That didn't work either, and I wondered what was going on. Was he going to whip me here, in my cell? Another chill raced down my back as I realized that up until now, my cell had been my refuge. All the torture had taken place in other rooms. Now the enemy was in my place, and there was no place left for me to run.

I thought wildly of running. Perhaps I could break and run through the prison. They might see me running and shoot. I might be able to get myself shot and killed. Or maybe I could just get shot and assigned to the prison hospital. Surely they couldn't torture me in the hospital!

Or could they? The idea of lying helpless while they toyed with open wounds — wounds that would leave scars, no matter what — was more than I wanted to deal with. Besides, the time I had tried running they had easily subdued me. They hadn't even had to draw their guns.

Maybe I could get hold of one of the guns they wore!

But maybe that was something they were hoping for, too.

"Sir?" I inquired at last.

"Permission to speak granted," he said coolly.

"Is there anything you want me to do, Sir?" I asked.

"Yes," he said. "I want you to learn. I want you to learn what to do without my having to bother telling you. — But I guess queers are a little stupid, so I'll tell you one last time. After that I'll expect you to respond without orders, unless you're told to do something different. You understand?"

"Sir! Yes, Sir!" I responded.

"Good. From now on, when one of us comes in, you're to strip immediately and come to parade rest."

"Sir! Yes, Sir!" I said.

As there was no further instruction, I did as I was told. When I stood naked before him in the small cell, he finally stopped leaning against the door and stood upright, himself coming to something like parade rest.

"Get down on your knees," he said.

I did so, figuring that I was going to get to suck his cock; then checking myself in my mind, I wondered why I was thinking about it in terms of 'getting to.'

"Kneel upright and put your hands behind your back, the same way you would at parade rest."

I did it.

He stepped forward so that his crotch was right in front of my face, about eight inches away. Slowly he began to massage his groin, and through the material of his pants I saw his big cock grow. Longer, thicker, much larger than I had imagined it standing in the shower. I figured it must be eight, nine, ten inches long! It was so thick that there was barely room for it in the trouser leg with his powerful thigh.

"Take one hand from behind you," he said, "and jerk yourself off!"

I took my right hand from behind me and grasped my cock. The feeling of my own hand on my own shaft was suddenly a totally new sensation as I knelt there, staring at this big Marine's huge tool through the tight-stretched material of his pants. I began to feel excited by the experience. My cock felt as though electric current was shooting through it, and hardening to stony stiffness. I jerked faster.

"See, sailor," he said. "You don't even need a whipping to get you up. Just a Marine in front of you. A Marine always makes a sailor's mouth water, doesn't he?"

I didn't know whether he wanted me to answer or not, but I rasped out: "Sir! Yes, Sir!" — Just in case.

"Now, tell me how queer you are."

I started telling him. I found that the words the sergeant had put in my mouth came out real easy, and when I finished them I started rattling off more. I didn't say anything original, but new ways to say it kept coming out, and I realized that what I was doing, inside myself, was begging for him to give me permission to come. No matter what I said, all that really mattered was that I get my rocks off, kneeling there in front of him, jerking my cock furiously and staring at his big hard-on.

"You're about ready," he said as I felt it happening. "So go ahead and shoot. But I want you to shoot it on my boots, an equal amount on each one, and I don't want a drop of it on the floor. If you spill any, I'll give you a hundred lashes!"

His last words took me over the top. I felt the flood pouring up and out, and I held my cock firmly, looking down and aiming it right at his left boot. White drops shot out like bullets, spattering and sticking to the shiny leather.

I moved my cock to the right, letting the next volley shoot onto his right boot. It wasn't as strong a shot, but it hit and stuck, and ran down the leather in milky white trickles. I shook with the force of it, aiming it, trying to figure out how I could stop the last weak drops from falling to the floor. Then I hit on the solution, and as the last big glob came pulsing out of my shaft, I shook it so that it flew and hit the boot!

My heart pounded, and I was breathing in great gasps. I felt sweat pouring off my forehead and trickling down my sides from my armpits. The smell of my own sweat was overpowering, and I realized it had been four days since I'd had a shower.

I felt my heart slow and the harsh reality of where I was came slowly back. I was still on my knees in front of the Marine, and he still stood there with an enormous erection. I slowly got myself back to an upright kneeling position, then put my hands back behind me.

"Good," he said. "You're starting to think a little like a slave. That's what I want. I want you to know what to do before I want it. Now, you think back; and figure out what you should do next!"

It only took me a moment to understand what he wanted. When he had whipped me, he'd jerked me off on the floor and made me lick it up. He obviously wanted me to lick it off his boots.

I brought my hands around in front of me and hunched my knees back, then lowered myself on my elbows to where I could get my face near his feet. Then I started licking my still-warm come off the shiny leather.

When I first contemplated the prospect that they might make me suck cock in prison, I figured it would make me throw up. The idea of semen pouring into your mouth is just too much for most American men. They grow up thinking that their tool is just for pissing until they get old enough to find out different first hand. By then they have the idea that it's something nasty, something you only stick into a cunt.

But my first taste of semen was just the end of a long session of terrors, and so I'd got past the worst of my reactions to it by having worse reactions to something else, the whipping. Now I found I could lick it up without more than a shudder, even if it was my own.

I was curious about the taste, because I'd always imagined it would be something really horrible. But, to my surprise, I found out that it wasn't awful at all. It was not much different than the taste of soap (which my grandmother washed my mouth out with when I swore!), only it was effervescent.

No, not really effervescent. I knew at once that it wasn't bubbles I was feeling in my mouth, but sperm cells, thrashing their little tails and shooting to every corner of my mouth, under my tongue, into my throat, between my teeth; trying to fight their way into where the tooth joins the gum. It was like bubbles, but like very tiny bubbles; and I knew they were alive, there in my mouth!

The taste of the semen on the dirty floor had been mingled with the taste of dirt in the untended room. But the taste of it on the dark corporal's boots was mingled with boot polish, and that was something else. It wasn't so much a separate taste as it was the aroma of leather that reeked out of the boots so near my face. It brought back the memory of the black leather razor strop and the whipping, and I found myself getting hard again.

I licked his boots clean, making sure there was not a drop of my come left.

I knew that he meant it about the hundred lashes, and though I didn't think I could live through them, I knew that if he said he would do it, he could; and that the sergeant would make sure it didn't kill me, or leave any marks. I didn't want a hundred lashes from the dark corporal, no matter how much it turned me on!

I got back up to my kneeling position, right in front of his big cock, which was still hard, and which he was still rubbing. I wondered if now he would have me suck him off.

But he didn't. He just stuck out each boot to make sure it was clean and shiny, then turned around and left.

I knelt there for a long time; then, not quite knowing what I was doing, I jacked off again.

But that time I didn't lick it up!

I wondered if he would come back, or if the three of them would open the door soon and march me to the showers, and then to another whipping. But as the time passed my knees got tired of the floor and I got up, and after more time I remembered my discovery that calisthenics would loosen the muscles and ease the pain. My clothes, unchanged for several days, looked unappealing, so I stayed naked and did my exercises, and after that I felt better.

Breakfast, lunch, and dinner arrived, but I still wasn't taken out, and neither were my dishes. The last cleaning my cell had had was when I'd been at the medical examination. I figured they'd have to change things soon, but there certainly was no reason to complain. Change, in my position, was likely to be painful.

I slept, awoke the next morning, emptied my bowels as usual, and waited.

I was still naked, and now I noticed that I was warm. Not uncomfortably so, but I realized that if I put my stale clothes on, I would be. I splashed some water on my face and under my arms from the tap, then dried myself on my blanket. After a while the door opened and the red-headed corporal stepped in, closing the door behind him.

I knew what he wanted, and I was already part way there. I stepped toward him, feeling his eyes on my naked, shaved body, and went down on my knees in front of him, putting my hands behind me.

He laughed softly and reached for his crotch. His prick got hard almost instantly, and so did mine. I wondered if he wanted me to jack off as well. Then, instinctively, I knew he did. I reached around and took my cock in my hand.

"I bet you can almost taste it, can't you, sailor boy?"

"Sir! Yes, Sir!" I said.

"Well, good!" he drawled. "Tell me about it!"

I started telling him, first with the words the sergeant had taught me, then with variations, telling him over and over how queer I was; and then I started telling him how much I wanted to taste my own come splattered all over his boots. I saw a wet spot appear on his pants, at the end of his hard cock, and he jacked himself faster and faster. I felt sure he was going to shoot, and I was equally sure that if he did, he wanted me to take it in my mouth. So I started telling him how much I wanted to taste *his* come.

"You're gonna get to, sailor boy," he said. "You're gonna get to!"

I felt my own orgasm coming on. I slowed my fist, waiting for him to pull out his cock.

"You're gonna get to," he said, noticing my slowing. "But not yet! Now keep on, I want my boots cleaned!"

I speeded up my jerking, felt myself growing close, closer. Then I felt his hand grab the back of my head and he shoved my face against his crotch. I opened my mouth and felt his hard cock with my lips, through the rough material of his pants. Then I felt the come boiling up and coursing through its channel and shooting out the head.

I tried to pull away so that I could see where to shoot it on his boots, but he held my head fast against his prick. All my load spattered, but I couldn't see where. The thought of a hundred lashes made me shudder, and I could tell the corporal knew just what I was thinking, because he laughed.

Then he let my head go and smiled down at me broadly, his white teeth flashing out of his pink freckled face.

"Made a mess, boy," he said, delighted. "You get punished when you do that, you know?"

"Sir! Yes, Sir!" I snapped, gulping.

"I'll give you a choice, boy. A hundred stripes later, or something right now. Which is it gonna be?"

The fear of a hundred lashes made up my mind for me.

"Sir! Now, Sir!"

"Good!" he said. "Now, first clean up the mess."

I got down and licked off his boots, then went over the rough concrete floor with my tongue, getting every drop of come that I could find. Finally there was no way I could pretend to be looking for any more, so I knelt back up.

The corporal walked around in back of me, and a moment later I heard the clink of metal and felt my hands bound behind me with a pair of handcuffs.

"Turn around," he said.

I scooted slowly around on my knees to face him.

Slowly, as he did everything, and with obvious pleasure in my seeing him do it, he took off his heavy leather belt. For a moment he stroked his still-hard rod, then he hauled off with the belt and let me have it across the chest.

If he had hit me in the ribs he might have broken them, but he was too skilled to do anything like that. He struck straight across the upper chest, landing the blow on the part protected by muscle, and right across the nipples. With my hands bound behind me there was not even any danger of my shoulders slumping forward to take part of the blow.

He laughed lightly, stroked his cock again, and delivered another stroke to my chest.

"Come on," he said. "Let's hear some more about how much you want to suck my big dick!"

He swung again and the agony seared across my chest, landing with the edge right on my tits. I started babbling what he wanted to hear, and kept on as long he kept whipping me. I figured later that it was only ten or twelve strokes, but it was bad enough that I ended up begging and pleading and crying about how much I wanted that big prick in my mouth, shooting my mouth full of his come.

When he finished whipping me he was sweating and the armpits of his shirt were soaked. He walked around in back of me, undid the handcuffs, and left. I crumpled over, grasping my aching chest, resting my head on the floor.

My cock was hard, all right, but I didn't care.

The third day I figured I would get to lick the sergeant's boots. But now they had me going, and they weren't going to let me figure out anything ahead of time. I had thought the calisthenics would restore me a little, but after my chest had been whipped, I found I couldn't do about half the exercises I had learned in boot camp. I would have to wait. — But it was the third day after my rest, and suddenly my old routine was restored. The three Marines were there in the morning; I was marched to the showers and scalded, then on to the room with the wooden table. The only difference was that I was marched through the halls of the prison naked, and when I got back to my cell, there were no clothes there, nor any blankets on the bed.

But after what happened in the room with the table, I didn't much care about blankets or clothes. Whatever they wanted of me they would have!

I was burning with the shower and somehow ashamed of my nakedness. Not that there had been anyone in the halls to see me; but somehow to be marched around without clothes seemed like being treated as an animal. And that, no doubt, is what they intended me to feel like.

I was ordered up on the table and the two corporals held my shoulders. The sergeant ran his hand over my body softly, almost lovingly, before he brought the leather strop down. I don't know whether he was being soft on me or hitting as hard as the dark corporal had. I was beyond making comparisons. It hurt, and I twitched with the pain, and that was all that counted to anyone, them or me.

Ten lashes, the soft stroking of the sergeant's hand, and then a new order.

"Get up and stand at the foot of the table, parade rest," the sergeant said.

I did as I was told, wondering what was going to happen. The red-headed corporal moved behind me, and I felt the handcuffs bind my wrists. The dark corporal came around in front of me and fastened the sharpened alligator clips to my tits. The pain was worse than it had been when he did it before, because my chest had been whipped the day before. Then the three of them went over and stood against the wall.

The two corporals peeled off their shirts, and the three of them stood, stripped to the waist. It was then I noticed how hot it was. How it had been getting hotter each day. All three of the Marines were now sweating, and the strong smell of them welled up and filled the room. I was sweating, too, but I'd thought it was from the beating. Now I realized that the room was actually hot. More than that, I realized that my cell had also been getting hotter. It was one reason I had not put my clothes on that first time.

"You're doing very well," the sergeant said, raising his thick eyebrows in an expression meant to compliment me. "You've learned to follow orders. But I want more than that out of you. I don't want you to have to think before you obey me. I want your body to obey me of its own volition, without having to go through your mind. I'm going to train you so well that you have no will but mine. I'm going to take you down to a level where my word alone will be as good as a thing done to you. I'm going to remake you so that when I say 'wake,' you will wake, and when I say 'sleep,' you will sleep. And when I say 'come,' you will come; just as if I'd put you on that table and whipped you all day. The first lesson toward that end you will get now. I'm going to stand here, and I'm going to snap my fingers, and I'm going to say 'come;' and then I'm going to give you five minutes to do it. If you don't do it, I'm going to let my friend here with the heavy hand work you over a little more."

He nodded toward the dark corporal and then turned back to me, smiling.

"Oh, you don't have to do it by will power," he said. "Not this time. You can use anything in the room you want. Hump the table. Rub your prick against the wall. Get down on the floor and do it. Just remember that you have to do it whenever I tell you to. That's what's important. The automatic shooting will come later."

"*Come!*"

I didn't know what to do. My cock was hard with fear, but my hands were bound!

I tried bending double so that I could get my cock between my knees or thighs. That felt good, but I couldn't move it. I tried scrabbling up on the table, so that I could fuck against the wood; but I couldn't do it with my hands bound. I went to the wall, but the old cracking paint cut at me. Finally I got down on the wooden floor and started humping the dry, dirty boards, rubbing back and forth with my cock between my belly and them.

But it was hopeless. I couldn't do it! I was too scared and helpless and uncoordinated. I heard them laughing at me, particularly the redhead, and that made it worse. The time ran out and I started babbling and pleading, and the sergeant slapped me across the face, reminding me that I was *never* to plead before the punishment. Then they took the clips off my tits, the handcuffs off my wrists, and I was ordered up on the table.

I was shaking with fear as I felt the dark corporal slide his club up my ass and the sergeant and the redhead pin my shoulders. I cried out as he crushed my balls, and again as he pulled my cock straight down. Then I felt the rush of emptiness as he pulled the stick out of my asshole and the overwhelming fear as the strop whirred through the air and landed on my butt.

When he had given me ten lashes I was again ordered up, handcuffed, and the clips put on my tits. The three of them leaned up against the wall, sweating and smiling, and the sergeant said, *"Come!"*

I fell to my knees, then to the floor, and started rubbing my cock against the boards. I shoved and pushed and fucked with all my might, but the only reward I got was a splinter in the head of my prick. And when my five minutes were up, I was up again, uncuffed, unclipped, and back on the table. The club this time wasn't slid into my ass, it was shoved, and there wasn't any trace of pleasure in it.

Another ten lashes, back up, and I wasn't even in my body anymore. My mind was far away, dazed, uncomprehending. It took a long while for me to figure out that the sergeant hadn't ordered me to come, he had ordered me to my knees instead. And he was saying something soft and sympathetic to me, not giving me orders.

"It'll take you a little while to learn that trick, Rover; but you'll learn it, don't worry. A good slave learns every trick his Master teaches him. A bad slave is no slave at all, you understand?"

"Sir! Yes, Sir!" I rasped out.

"You want to be a good slave, don't you?"

"Sir! Yes, Sir!"

"You want to surrender your will completely to me and have no thoughts but my thoughts, don't you?"

"Sir! Yes, Sir!"

"And if I want my friends to be happy, you'll work to make them happy, too, won't you?"

"Sir! Yes, Sir!"

"Good. Now I want you to say: 'Your humble queer slave wants only your pleasure, Sir!'"

"Your humble queer slave wants only your pleasure, Sir!"

"Good! You'll think about the way you said that tonight when you're asleep. You never used the word 'I,' and you never will again, on pain of special punishment. From now on, you have no self at all. You will refer to yourself only in terms of me. As 'your humble slave,' as 'your worthless queer slave,' and things like that. You will forget that you ever had any self. You understand?"

"Sir! Yes, Sir!"

"Good. Now, I think it's about time we gave you some reward for all that you've learned. It would make me happy to see you rewarded. Do you think you deserve a reward?"

I started to speak, but there was just enough extra care in his voice to give away the trap. I thought furiously, pushing down the fog of pain in my mind.

"Sir!" I said. "The only possible reward for your worthless slave is your pleasure."

He smiled at that. He was pleased. He nodded.

"Come here to me," he said, calling me over with his finger, the way one gestures to a child. "Stay on your knees, but come here."

I crawled across the floor, realizing as I did so that my hands were cuffed behind my back and that the pain in my tits from the alligator clips was barely noticeable, so awful was the pain of my back and ass. I reached the position in front of the sergeant, my face inches away from his crotch.

He reached down and unzipped his pants.

This is it! I thought. Finally my fears were going to be fulfilled, and now there was no fear left. The idea of having the sergeant's cock in my mouth was only remotely distasteful, somewhere way off at the back of my mind. It represented only a time and space where there was no whipping.

He pulled his cock out, and I was surprised to see that it was soft. Even so, it was big. A thick, long, dark cock, all brown, with curly black hairs sticking out from the fly and growing a little way up the shaft. The head was smooth, like a big purple plum, and the large slit at the end of it glistened.

"Tell me about it, slave," the sergeant whispered.

"Sir!" I said, and I found that I could barely speak. "I . . . your humble, stupid slave, Sir, your queer slave, Sir, wants to suck your dick, Sir!"

"Why?" whispered the sergeant.

"Because it will . . . because it *might* give you pleasure, Sir!"

He nodded, then took his cock in his hand and slapped me across the face with it a couple of times. The musky smell of his crotch overpowered me. I felt my cock so hard I thought it would burst, and the splinter in the head was like some fabulous jewel, not hurting, but burning with extra pleasure.

"Ready?" he asked.

"Sir, Yes, Sir! Please, Sir!"

He leaned back against the wall and let a stream of hot, bright yellow piss shoot out of his cock. He pissed down onto my cock and balls, sprayed it back and forth across my belly, working up my chest, and finally he let me have it full in the face.

Unthinking, I closed my mouth and eyes against the stream. As soon as I did, it stopped. Then I felt the sergeant's thumb and forefinger slip past the barrier of my lips, slide neatly to either side of my mouth, outside my teeth, and insert themselves behind my molars on either side. My lips were stretched painfully, but I knew he didn't care. He was only interested in getting at the back of my mouth, where his finger and thumb could push in behind my teeth, prying my upper and lower teeth apart and forcing my mouth wide open. Then I felt and tasted the stream of hot piss shoot into my open mouth.

I didn't know what to expect. I had never even thought of having piss in my mouth. I found that I somehow expected it to be salty, but it was not. It was mildly sweet, and strongly musky, like the muskiness of sweat. It tasted as if some kind of strange and concentrated sweat were being poured into my mouth, and the aroma of it, not the same somehow as the smell that comes up when you are pissing, filled my nostrils.

"Swallow it!" the sergeant said.

I realized that I had been letting it pour back out of my mouth and down my chest. I tried to swallow, but I found I couldn't. I started to gag.

The sergeant stopped his flow and took his hand away from my mouth.

"It'll be easier to swallow without my fingers in your mouth," he said. "And you will swallow it! The trouble you are having is that you're going about it wrong. I don't want you drooling all over yourself like an idiot. You have to take my cock in your mouth, and when I piss, you have to suck on it, like a soda straw, swallowing at the same rate you would if you were drinking out of a fountain. You understand? If you don't understand, it's back to the table until you do!"

"Sir!" I gasped. "Sir! Yes, Sir!"

"Good. Now, take it!"

He stepped closer to me and put his big prick in my mouth. I felt the close-cut hairs on the back of my neck rise, wondering if I'd be able to do what he wanted, wondering how long I'd be whipped by the dark corporal if I didn't. I fastened my mouth on his cock and started to suck the way I would if it were a soda straw, and the warm stream came, flowing into my mouth as fast as I could swallow, filling my nose with its musky taste.

He'd spent a lot of his stream on my body, so there wasn't a lot to take. For that I was grateful. It seemed to me that drinking the sergeant's piss was a big accomplishment, a prize I'd won, and with which I had bought time off the wooden table. He put his tool back into his pants after shaking a couple of drops into my face, then turned to the redhead.

"Your turn," he said.

I realized then that I was going to have to take it from all three of them. But I didn't panic or struggle. I knew it was coming, and the only thing I could do was take it, buying more time when I wasn't being whipped.

The redhead stood in front of me and pulled his cock out, and I saw that there was something about him I hadn't known. His long, thin tool, with a head bigger than the shaft, was uncircumcised. It was a pink cock, with stiff red pubic hair sticking out of the pants, and there were some freckles on the smooth shaft. When he pulled the foreskin back the head was moist, and bright purple in color, smooth as satin and shiny.

He put the head in my mouth, took my head in his hands, and let the stream flow. His piss tasted a little different than the sergeant's had, and it came in a harder stream so that I had to struggle to swallow it as quickly as my mouth filled. There was so much of it that I figured he'd saved it up for me. When he finished he made me lick the head of his cock clean, then he laughed and put it back in his pants.

The dark corporal's cock was big and thick and long and very wrinkled and dark. I knew it must be huge when it was hard, but looking at the great, meaty head of the thing, brown like a deep suntan, I couldn't imagine how it could get much bigger. I was afraid that I wouldn't be able to get it into my mouth, but I was able to. It filled my mouth very nicely, and then the steam of piss came out.

I nearly choked. Not on the sheer volume of it, which was bad enough, but on the taste. The other two men had tasted like musky sweat, only sweet. The dark corporal's piss tasted foul and bitter. I was sure I would gag, but there was no way that anything could come back up my throat. I wasn't so much swallowing what he was shooting into my mouth as holding my throat open and letting a hose pour down it.

At the end, the dark corporal stopped the flow abruptly, pulled his cock out of my mouth, and pissed the last of his load over my head and in my face. The foul smell and taste of it filled my nostrils, my mouth, and hung on me like some evil perfume.

"That's what it tastes like when you eat some special things the night before," the dark corporal said, instructively. "What you just got was last night's asparagus. Maybe you'll learn to like it!"

The taste and smell was so foul that I knew that I was going to vomit.

There was certainly enough in me to puke! I had taken two and a half very full bladders, and my belly was tight full. I felt my gorge rising, but the sergeant spoke:

"Well, faggot, you've had your little treat! Now it's time to get back to work. You've still got some more lashes coming to you!"

Something must have happened in my body chemistry, because the thought of the whipping kept me from puking. I moved docilely as they uncuffed me, took the clips off, put the club up my ass, crushed my balls again, and then, taking the billy club out and pulling my cock straight down, started in on another thirty lashes, this time the privilege of the redhead, who'd so far been left out.

I figured that I had done all right since the last thirty lashes were not from the dark corporal.

Six

I did puke when I got back to my cell, and it was worse than drinking their piss had been. The foul taste of the dark corporal's asparagus piss was mixed with the acid from my stomach, and the whole batch came up so fast that it shot out through my nose as well as my mouth and fixed the smell in a way that I couldn't get rid of.

I fastened my lips to the faucet of my little wash basin and drank as much water as I could, washing my mouth and nose out and wondering what my body would do. Was piss dangerous, I wondered? I figured the best thing to do was wash myself out, so I kept drinking water.

My cell had been cleaned and the sheets changed, but there were no fresh clothes for me. It was also much hotter than it had been before, and I figured this was going to be another turn of the screw. Bad food, torture, and now heat. I was beginning to wish for a nice vacation on Devil's Island!

I kept drinking water, as much as I could hold, and eventually I started pissing; but I think I sweated as much as I pissed. I hurt so much I couldn't even think about my calisthenics; and when I finally went to sleep, I dreamed about being whipped and drinking piss.

The next morning I was drenched in sweat and I had a headache from sleeping in the dry heat. My bowels moved and my guards came for me, dressed neat and clean in their pressed Marine uniforms, looking as happy and as comfortable as a Marine can look.

They marched me naked through the halls, which I gratefully found cool, and gave me my usual scalding shower. The sergeant played with my ass and my cock again, so when we started marching down the halls, I was hard, a thing that made it doubly humiliating.

They didn't take me to the room with the wooden table, but marched me through a cell block full of prisoners who looked like they were in better shape than I was. I felt their eyes on me, but the humiliation only made me get harder. I knew the sergeant was getting into my mind and making me do what he wanted, making me respond the way he wanted me to respond.

When one of the prisoners whistled, I felt my body go red all over, even redder than the scalding shower had left it.

We came to a door that looked like the entrance to an office, and I found myself escorted into a lounge. It was pretty much the kind of lounge that one sees for noncoms, but was a little better fitted out than usual. There were big, brown leather chairs and sofas, a pool table, a card table with a light over it, a great big color television, a door labeled 'Men,' another door leading to a kind of cloakroom, and a section with a movie screen and a projector. There was also a big refrigerator in the corner, and the sergeant headed right for it.

The lounge was as hot as my cell had been, so there was a special kind of torture when the sergeant reached into the refrigerator and pulled out three cans of beer. He tossed two of them to the corporals and pulled the tab on the one for himself, tossing the little metal tab into a waste basket near the door of the cloakroom. Smiling at me, he took a long, slow swig of the cold beer.

I licked my lips involuntarily, and he laughed.

"You'll get some of it," he said. "After I'm finished with it!"

One of the corporals went to the movie projector, opened a can of film that lay next to it, and put the reel on the sprocket. He threaded the film carefully, turned the projector on, and tested it. When he was satisfied he nodded.

"See that big, soft chair, directly in front of the screen?" the sergeant asked.

"Sir! Yes, Sir!" I said.

"I want you to go sit in it," he said. "We're going to show you some dirty movies, and I want you to be nice and comfortable while you're watching them. I want you to play with that cock of yours while you're watching, and I want you to get right to the point of coming; but I don't want you to come until I tell you to. Understand?"

"Sir! Yes, Sir!" I said.

I went and sat in the big, soft leather chair. It seemed to wrap itself around me, caressing my naked body with its soft leathern coolness, and the smell of it was incredibly exciting. I realized that it was probably the bootlicking that had made the leather sexual for me; then I realized that I had always liked the smell of leather in new boots and belts and hats.

The sergeant and the redhead drew chairs up to either side of me, facing me rather than the screen, about four feet ahead of me on the diagonals. They then stripped to the waist, sat down in their chairs, and started playing with themselves through their trousers. Behind me I heard the motor of the projector whir, then the lights went out and the movie started. My cock, which had begun to go soft, got rock hard again.

A brief screen credit in block letters proclaimed the film to be a Marine training film on interrogation of military prisoners during time of war. I wondered if this film was actually listed in a booklet somewhere with a number assigned to it and everything; but I didn't really care what the Marines used for training films, because I knew that this film was really meant for me, and anyone unlucky enough to be in the same fix I was.

The lights came up on a room much like the one we were in, a noncom lounge. The film was grainy, and the sound was hollow and amateurish; but then, a lot of training films were like that.

The door opened and a young man walked in, a Navy man, a second-class petty officer. He was followed by three Marine M.P.'s, a sergeant and two corporals. It looked familiar. They shut the door.

He was dark, rather than blonde like me. His hair was black and he had brown eyes. His nose was small but well-formed, and he had a short, bushy mustache as black as his hair. His jaw was firm, his lips full and sensual. He was slighter of build than me, but it was a very good build, with firm arms and a round ass. His chest was thicker than mine. All in all, he was an attractive man, the kind who could have taken the girls in bars away from me every time, and frequently did by sheer masculine bravado.

The three Marines with him were pulled from the same mold as my guards, but all three of them were light in coloring and complexion. They reminded me of those blond Germans Hitler always said he was breeding for, despite Hitler's being a dark little runt!

He came and stood looking straight at the camera, the Navy man, and one of the Marines said: "What's Navy scum good for?"

"Sucking cock, Sir!" the Navy man said.

"What else?"

"Getting fucked, Sir!"

"What else?"

"Anything you want, Sir!"

"Take your clothes off, faggot!"

Slowly, deliberately, the black-haired, brown-eyed young man stripped, dropping his uniform on the floor, staring all the while intently into the camera.

His chest was thickly furred with black, curly hair. His belly was smooth, but the black hair began again right under his navel and ran in a thin line down to the middle to where it spread out in a thick patch of pubic hair. His cock was as large as mine, but no bigger; but he was uncircumcised, and that always makes a cock look bigger. As soon as he got his clothes off, he began to get hard.

One of the Marines came over and stood beside him, sideways to the camera.

"Get down on your knees," he said.

The sailor obeyed.

The Marine opened his pants and pulled out a big, semi-hard cock. He put one hand behind the boy's head and pulled his face close; then he rubbed his cock all over the boy's face.

The sailor's face began to change. His look of obedience changed to one of desire. His mouth went slack and he licked his lips; but he didn't try to take the big cock; he just let the Marine rub it in his face.

The Marine undid his belt, opened his pants all the way, and pulled down his skivvies, revealing the full size of his cock and his large, pendulous balls, wreathed and tufted with twisted blond hair.

"Lick my balls!" the Marine commanded.

The sailor put his face between the big man's legs and began lapping at the huge balls, letting them fall wetly across his face, working faster as he went. He grew more and more excited as he licked. His cock was like an iron, almost upright against his stomach.

"Now you've got it, " I heard my sergeant say, and I realized that I was jacking my own cock rapidly, really getting into the scene I was watching. "But don't shoot till I tell you, remember!"

"Now suck my cock!" the Marine in the movie said.

The sailor slid his tongue up the big shaft, then took the end of it into his mouth. He sucked and sucked, working on the head I couldn't tell how, then moving his head back and forth, plunging the big tool deeper and deeper into his throat. The Marine took hold of his head on both sides and began to move his hips, plunging his cock in forcefully as the sailor sucked.

The sailor took hold of the Marine's legs, below the level where the pants hung, and held on tight as the Marine fucked his mouth. Harder and harder the Marine rammed his cock in till I wondered if he would fuck the back of the boy's skull out.

Then I saw the Marine stiffen, heard him roar out a groan of raging pleasure, and abruptly he pulled the sailor's face away from his cock. He held the boy by his black hair, just beyond the reach of the cock, and with his other hand held his cock as it shot right into the sailor's face.

Gobs of white semen shot from the engorged end of his tool, splattering on the sailor's nose, on his cheeks, and sticking in big white drops in his stiff black mustache. The sailor held his mouth open and tried to catch some of it, and some of it did shoot into his mouth, and he licked his lips hungrily. But even though he reached out with his tongue toward the Marine's shooting cock, he couldn't catch even most of it. It coated his face with dripping lines of sticky white, and after a moment, the Marine, finished with his coming, laughed.

I felt my own load coming to a head. I thought about what they might do to me if I came, but it didn't seem worth delaying any longer. They would do to me what they wanted anyway, and I couldn't hold back. I jerked faster and faster, and stole a glance at the sergeant as the Marine of the screen took his come-covered cock and wiped it all over the sailor's face, rubbing the semen into the mustache especially.

Abruptly there was a shadow on the screen and a powerful hand grabbed my wrist and wrenched it away from my cock. Even my brief glance was enough to tell me that the sergeant knew what I was doing, and that he had nodded the dark corporal into action. I moaned with frustration more than fear as the dark corporal yanked me up out of my leather cushions, twisted my arms behind me, and put on the handcuffs. Then he threw me down again, my hands bound behind me, nestled in the soft cushions, my cock aching for release.

The redhead got up and walked over to me, laughing a huge guffaw as he approached. He opened his pants and took out his long, thin, uncut cock.

"Want to suck it now, faggot?" he asked.

"Sir! Yes, Sir!" I responded.

He laughed and put it back in, then went back to his chair.

"Keep watching the movie," the sergeant said quietly.

On the screen the dark-haired sailor was still kneeling, his face smeared with come. The first Marine had moved away from him and sat down in a big leather chair, not too different from the one in which I was sitting. The other two Marines now proceeded to strip. The sailor still had his raging hard-on; but he was careful not to touch it, and I got the point of what was going on. He held his hands almost in back of him, resting against the sides of his firm ass as if he knew a wrong move would put them promptly into handcuffs.

The two blond Marines, both of them smooth-bodied with clearly delineated muscles all over, came over and pulled the sailor up to his feet. They moved him over to a leather sofa and pushed him down, unresisting, on top of the sofa back. One of them lifted his left leg so that he straddled the sofa back, his head at one end, his ass at the other, one leg over the back, the other resting on the seat. The other Marine grabbed him under the armpits and pulled him along so that his head hung a little over the end.

He offered no resistance, but complied with their handling of him as if he were a mannequin, accustomed to being moved into different positions and left that way. One of the Marines lifted his head and set it down facing the camera, as if to be sure the viewer could see his face and its expressions.

Then the same Marine moved his head again, lifted it by his black hair, and said: "Tell us!"

"I want to suck you, Sir!" the sailor said. "And I want you to fuck me, Sir!"

The Marine smiled and stuck his hardening cock into the sailor's mouth. The sailor started sucking, and in a minute the Marine started pumping his tool in and out. But after a couple of minutes more, he pulled his cock out and signaled to his partner to come forward. The second Marine, already hard, stuck his cock into the sailor's mouth and started fucking it, while the first Marine, smiling at the camera and displaying an enormous erection, went around to the other end of the couch, hitched one leg over the back, and with no preamble, stuck the head against the boy's ass and shoved it in.

I could see the sailor writhe and his hands clench at the leather as the big tool drove in. I could hear him scream, as best he could with that other big cock plunging into his throat. I felt my asshole tighten in sympathetic fear. But I also felt my cock throb, and I found that my legs had moved up and were caressing my cock. Anything to try and bring it to orgasm!

My sergeant got up and came over to me. I didn't know what he was going to do, but I was whimpering now with fear and lust. I felt that I would do anything if he would only allow me to come! He reached down and gently moved my legs downward away from my cock. I couldn't ask him for anything, but I moaned at his touch.

He slid his hand gently up my leg and cradled my balls, squeezing them, massaging them. Then, as I twisted with pleasure, he let go of them and reached up and undid his pants. He pulled them down, skivvies and all, and I saw his cock, and for the first time, his hairy, huge balls. He was hard now, and it was a big, rock-hard cock, long and thick and dark. The slit at the end glistened and dripped a small glassy bead of pre-come.

I was only half aware of the scene on the screen now with my sergeant's real cock right in front of my face. But the sound of the Marines panting and grunting as they rammed their cocks into the hapless sailor and the grunts of pain and fear from the sailor flooded my mind and turned my body into a hurricane of lust.

I felt, more than saw, the redhead come up and lift me from my chair and lower me to a kneeling position before the sergeant. My mind was a useless block in the way of my desires. I felt the redhead kneel behind me, between my wide-spread legs, and I felt his long cock slip between my legs and the head position itself against the opening of my asshole. I wanted to push my ass against it to help it in, but I didn't know if that was what they wanted me to do. I felt his hand slide around my hip, down my belly, and take hold of my cock. I felt as if I would scream with the pleasure of it. The Marines on the screen were pounding furiously into both ends of the sailor.

The sergeant stepped toward me and put his cock no more than an inch from my lips. I knew I could reach forward with my head and take it in my mouth; but if that was the wrong move, he might not let me come. It didn't occur to me that he might not anyway. All I could think about was doing whatever the sergeant wanted, so that he would let me come.

"Lick that little drop off," he said, just loud enough for me to hear him over the movie.

It was all I could do to control myself. I wanted to seize his cock with my mouth and suck it. I wanted to ram my ass down on top of the redhead's cock and feel it plunge into me the way the billy club had or his fingers. But I just stuck out my tongue and licked off the one clear drop of pre-come that glistened from the end of the sergeant's cock.

As I did it, I felt the corporal start to slide my cock back and forth. Slowly he masturbated me, building the awful explosion that I desired more than anything.

"Open your mouth," the sergeant said.

I did it, and he stepped a little closer.

"Don't suck it, " he said. "Just let it sit there in your mouth. Don't even move your tongue."

He put the big head of his cock into my mouth and rested it on my tongue. On the screen, the two Marines roared out as their orgasms hit almost simultaneously. My eyes moved to the screen and I watched their powerful, sweating bodies pounding in uncontrolled savagery into the black-haired sailor. The redhead speeded up his jerking on my cock.

"Come!" the sergeant commanded, using that tone of voice that he used when he told me to strip and lie on the table.

And I came! My balls tightened; my ass tightened around the head of the cock that pressed against it; involuntarily I sucked hard on the sergeant's cockhead; and I shot my load, wave after wave shooting out like hot lead from my stone-hard dick and spattering against the sergeant's brown trousers. If I was disobeying orders at that moment, I no longer knew it. I didn't know anything, except that I was a coming, just as the sergeant had told me to!

Later, when the film had run out and I was being marched back to my cell, I figured out that they had several counts on which to punish me. But I had apparently done what they wanted me to do, and that was more important than the basic orders. That made me proud.

Seven

Back in my cell I had time to calm down and think about what was happening to me. I had shot off on command, the way the sergeant wanted me to, and that had pleased him. I had responded to his commands for the most part, even though they'd had to cuff me. I was starting to respond the way they wanted me to.

But it seemed to me that I had felt a lot more than a desire to respond out of fear. The day before I had been a man doing whatever will keep him from being whipped. Suddenly I was a man who really wanted to please his captor. And I couldn't lie to myself. I really had wanted to suck his cock. I really had at the end wanted to get fucked by the redhead.

Why then hadn't they gone ahead and done it? Why had the sergeant pulled his cock back out of my mouth after I'd finished coming, and then the redhead stood up behind me and put his cock back in his pants? They had me responding like a faggot, they had me wanting the things I was supposed to want. What more was there? They had turned me queer, and that was that!

But the sergeant had said that was only the first part of my training. He said he was going to control my body directly, so that it responded without me as middle man. I felt as if that were already the case, but it was all up to the sergeant. And whatever he did, so long as it wasn't with a leather belt, I figured I would like it!

I sweated, I drank more water, and I ate lunch and dinner when they came. I tried calisthenics, but it was too damned hot; and after a while I went to sleep.

In the middle of the night, or at least when I was soundly asleep, the door opened and the sergeant came in. I was awake instantly, but still a little blurry. I stood at attention automatically, and responded willingly when he put his hand on my shoulder and forced me to my knees. I didn't think there was anything strange about it when he put his soft cock in my mouth and said: "I promised you some beer!" and made me drink all the piss he'd been saving up for me. I went straight back to sleep when he left, not even bothering to get a drink.

The next day they took me back to the lounge and stationed me in my soft leather chair, got out their beers, and started another training movie.

The cast was the same, and the things started the same way; so I was at first sure they were showing me the same movie over again. But I realized as the sailor started to suck cock that it was a different big, blond Marine who was fucking his mouth this time, one of those who had taken him on the couch in the previous film.

Things proceeded as before, and this Marine shot even more come all over the sailor's face, rubbing it into the mustache with special force. I wondered what it would be like to rub my cock against a mustache, and as I wondered it I rubbed my cock flat against my belly, where my shaved pubic hair was beginning to grow in again, short and prickly. It felt good, so I kept doing it, sliding it back and forth, while the other two Marines on the screen pulled the boy to his feet.

I expected them to throw him over the couch again, but they didn't. One of the corporals brought out a pair of black leather manacles lined with sheepskin and fastened them on his wrists; then they fastened the manacles with a sturdy clip to a rope that came down from the ceiling. I saw the rope tighten, pulled no doubt through a pulley by the Marine who was off-camera. Then the black-haired sailor had his arms jerked straight up, and with a third pull he was hauled by his arms off the floor, so that his feet were dangling about a foot off the ground.

The sight of his arms stretched above his head, his chest muscles stretched tight, his belly stretched smooth with the weight of his lower body, was a whole new level of excitement for me! I put my hand around my cock again and started stroking it. I was sure I could control myself this time, because I felt that the sergeant would let me come if I did as he wanted. And maybe, I felt, the sergeant would let me suck him all the way off.

On the screen, one of the Marines brought out a board about three feet long with two holes in it. It split up the middle, with a hinge on one end and a fastening on the other. They opened it, and one Marine held the boy's legs apart while the other fastened his ankles in it and locked it closed. It was a very effective way to keep his legs spread wide apart while he hung there.

One of the Marines took off his boots, and I had an idea of what was coming next. But he didn't take a lace out of it, the way the dark corporal had. Instead he took a little leather device with sharp points on the inside and double-wrapped it around both the sailor's balls and his cock. From this he lowered a piece of chain, and on the end of this he hung the boot.

I could see the little spikes cut into the kid's cock and balls, but he didn't even grimace; he just hung there and took it, his bright brown eyes staring into the camera. I wanted to come real bad but I just squeezed and kneaded my cock, wondering if they were going to do that to me.

Next one of the corporals walked around in back of the kid and slid his billy club up the kid's ass. Not hard, but slowly and deep. Now the sailor's face changed, and I could see waves of pleasure coming over him. The Marine pushed the club deeper and deeper up his ass, and finally he started to moan and twist his head back and forth, his brown eyes going all glassy.

The other corporal reached into his pocket and took out some big ball bearings, three-quarters of an inch across, and began dropping them, one by one, into the boot. The kid's moans turned into throaty cries, and the man with the ball bearings set the boot to swinging back and forth, just the way the dark corporal had made me swing his boot from my balls.

The sergeant in the movie appeared from the side of the screen with another device in his hand. It was a pair of alligator clips, much bigger and fiercer than the ones the dark corporal had used on me, and they were fastened together by a length of chain. He reached up and put them on the sailor's tits and I saw them bite in. The sailor's voice became a long, drawn-out yowl.

The corporal with the club started twisting it in a circle up the kid's ass, smiling at the additional rasp the voice took on. The sergeant reached up and began fastening heavy fishing sinkers to the chain between the alligator clips.

The sailor's whole body now twisted and writhed as he hung there. I couldn't tell whether he was in pain or in pleasure, but I knew what I was feeling from watching it. I squeezed my cock so hard it hurt, trying to hold on, trying to please my sergeant.

Then the sergeant on the screen said: "Come!" and I watched in amazement as the sailor's stretched, tortured cock throbbed in its binding and began to drip out long gouts of semen, each one as much as I was accustomed to shooting altogether. It was as if he'd been storing it up for months! Thick, white, viscous come poured straight down from the end of his cock into the boot that hung from it, along the chain.

He shook and trembled, and the shout that came out of his throat was so animal and raw I admired it. Whatever he was feeling, it was something beyond what I had ever felt from any kind of sex!

And then at my ear I heard my sergeant whisper: "Come!" and without hesitating, without needing to work my cock any more, I did. I felt like I was the boy on the screen, and my voice let go in my throat, not so raw as his, but responding to him. My balls shot tight against me, my ass tightened, and I shot, straight up, the droplets falling like white rain on my belly and my chest. My head went back and everything whited out. I didn't know anything except what my cock felt like as it shot.

I figured that was the end of it, when I came back from the never-never land of orgasm. But I was wrong. The movie on the screen continued, and I was left to sit and watch it, the semen cooling in wet drops on my belly and chest.

They slid the billy club out of the kid's ass; then they took off the alligator clips, revealing tiny drops of blood where the teeth had bit in. They took the boot, the chain, and the leather wrapping with the little spikes off his cock and balls. There were little marks on his cock, too, and little droplets of blood. Then they took the wooden frame off his feet and lowered him to the floor.

He didn't bother to look at the camera any more. His brown eyes were glazed now, and his body looked languorous, soft, like somebody floating in a swimming pool. He stood quietly as they undid the leather manacles, then pushed him over the back of a chair.

One of the corporals pulled a belt from his trousers, which he'd dumped on the floor. He doubled it, and without preliminary brought it down smartly across the kid's ass. It landed with a sharp crack, and the very sound of it brought blood back to my softened cock. I had lain on the wooden table so many times that even the thought of being whipped got me hard. But to actually see it from a position I'd never been in, that was too much! My cock got hard so quick that my balls, freshly emptied of their load, started to ache.

They whipped the black-haired sailor hard and for a long time. I sat fascinated, watching the red welts appear across his ass, the white lines of freshly delivered blows fading pink like a linear blush. He had coarse black hair growing on his legs, but it thinned as it came up his buttocks, and only thickened around the crack. Each blow made the crack of his ass contract abruptly, and I thought about what it would be like to have my cock in his asshole as the powerful muscles of his rear end contracted like that.

The Marine handed his belt over to his buddy, and the whipping continued. The first whipper was dripping with sweat, his muscular chest glistening, and he stood just right for all his best features to show. The second whipper didn't take long to match him, and he was a study in moist motion as well.

When the kid's ass glowed like a cherry the two Marines turned the chair he was bent over sideways, so that his back was visible as well as his ass. Then one of them shoved his big, hard dick up the kid's ass while the other proceeded to whip the boy across the back.

A part of me, buried deep inside, was responding to what I was seeing with righteous indignation. But most of me was responding on a purely physical, amoral level. I could only think of what it must be like to be fucking that sailor while his body tensed and writhed with the pain of the belt landing across his back. And I wondered, too, what it must be like to be fucked while being whipped!

I was jacking myself off furiously again, and this time I wasn't worried about coming. I had just come, after all, and I figured it would take a while for me to build up to it again.

But I wasn't taking into account the different life I had been living for some weeks now.

In the Navy I had been worked hard and constantly, and there wasn't much left over at the end of the day for sex. If I had the energy to jerk off into my sock at night, lying still in my rack, I figured I was doing okay.

But now, I had nothing to do that was not connected with sex or torture, and the sergeant had been working steadily to make the two of them one. Before I knew it, I felt the rush of another orgasm coming on me. I panicked, pulling my hand away from my cock, but knowing it was too late, and feeling the white hot load come boiling up, like lava from a volcano. I looked around from the screen, wordlessly imploring my sergeant for help as I felt myself shoot.

But my sergeant had planned this, just like everything else. As I felt the semen shoot out of my cock, I saw him standing just behind my chair, and I saw his upraised arm with the leather belt in it. I knew, even as my load shot upward in splattering drops, that his belt was about to land across my chest.

I felt the warm drops of come hit me at almost the same second as his belt landed, flat across my body, the edge cutting across my nipples. The pleasure of my orgasm blended with the pain of the belt, and my body couldn't tell the two apart. I groaned and shouted as it hit, and I clenched my fists at my sides, holding on to scraps of sanity as the belt landed again and again, and I continued to shoot. My cock raged, my balls ached, and the pleasure poured through my chest as he whipped me!

Whether I lost consciousness or not I don't know. I only remember the black-haired sailor on the screen bringing me back to awareness with his screaming. The man who was fucking him had grabbed his arms and twisted them behind him, then pulled him to a standing position, the big cock still up his ass. The other Marine, the one who had been using the belt on his back, started whipping him across the chest, the way the sergeant had been whipping me. The pain of the belt landing where the alligator clips had bit into his tits was too much for him, and the black-haired sailor had started to scream.

He'd also started to come, more semen pouring from his semi-hard organ and splattering on the legs of the Marine who was whipping him.

I groaned, not knowing what I was supposed to do, not knowing whether it was possible to be turned on any more. I had just felt what the boy on the screen was feeling. It was as if everything had been reversed. Now he was responding to me as pornography!

But that was crazy, I thought wildly!

I was here and alive and real, and he was only a film! What was happening on the screen was something that had happened a long time before.

My sergeant and my two corporals started laughing behind my chair.

Then, on the screen, the sergeant and the two corporals who held the black-haired sailor prisoner also started laughing, and turned to look at the camera.

They looked straight at me! The hair on the back of my neck began to stand up, and I felt as if madness were coming on.

But I had been eating poor food, being whipped a lot, and had just had two orgasms. There wasn't any room in my brain for madness. I felt everything slipping away, blackness coming on, and I fainted.

Eight

The prick of a needle being jabbed into my arm brought me out of my faint. I heard the sergeant telling me to keep still, and felt the dull pain of fluid being injected into my vein; then the needle was withdrawn; there was a stinging as alcohol was rubbed on the puncture; then it was quiet.

I tried to slip again into the blackness where I'd been hiding. It was nice and safe there in unconsciousness, and I wanted to go back there. But as I felt myself going down the slide and plunging into that refreshing darkness, the sharp smell of ammonia under my nose brought me abruptly back, and I was once again in the lounge, nestled in my big brown leather chair.

The screen was blank and the movie-projector silent. My guards were dressed and looked orderly. There was no sign of a corpsman, nor could I detect any trace of a hypodermic needle. I wondered for a moment if I had dreamed that part of it, then realized that they might want me to wonder about it. I remembered the weird sensation of the men in the movie responding to what was happening to me. It had been as if I were the porno movie, and they were the spectators.

More tampering with my reality, I realized. More unsettling of my mind.

Well, that was what it was all about, wasn't it? I had come into the prison with a firm conviction that I was a nice, straight, heterosexual male. The conviction most men have about themselves and the one on which they base most of their assumptions about themselves. If you can jar that conviction loose, then you have got them by the short hairs, and there's not a thing they can do about it!

And they had not only got me by the short hairs, they had cut them off! So here I was, thinking queer and holding on to what little there was of my 'self' by trying to do a good job at whatever my sergeant set me to. The short hairs were starting to grow in again, but now they were something different than they had been before. I wondered if I would be able to regain my heterosexual desires once I was out and not under their control any longer. I wondered if I would want to; and that really frightened me. It was one thing for them to control me in the Brig, it was another to think of my mind being permanently reshaped to think the way the government wanted me to think.

I think I would have laughed as I lay there if the sergeant would have approved of it. The very idea of my country, *my* country, the 'Land of the Free,' doing a thing like this — spending the money it must be costing the government to do this: it was ludicrous! What would the American public think if it knew this kind of thing went on?

But then the sergeant had made it quite clear that I would be so changed that I would be unable to let anybody know what had happened to me. But changed in ways that I couldn't point to or use to back up my assertions.

While all these things were happening to me, it never occurred to me to consider what training I had undergone as part of the 'regular' Navy. What kind of training was standard for anyone in the military? I hadn't exactly enjoyed boot camp, but while I was being whipped, it never occurred to me that the endless hours of calisthenics, the marching, the barracks life, the lack of privacy and the verbal abuse were only different in degree from what I was now experiencing more physically.

I've learned a lot since then, both about myself and about the way the government manipulates men's sexual desires in order to control them. The more you can repress people, the more you can count on their loyalty. The sex drive is so powerful that it has to have an outlet. How much better, from a government point of view, if the sex drive is tuned to Leadership rather than Love!

If you can make that change in a man, you haven't got a man any more, you've got a Marine whose sex drive is totally at the disposal of his superior officers.

The sergeant watched me like a hawk, his eyes almost glowing with expectation. What was in the needle? I wondered.

But I didn't feel any changes in my body, so I figured it was useless to speculate. If something was going to happen, it would happen.

After a while the sergeant smiled. I didn't feel any different, but whatever he was waiting for must have happened. He told me to get up and I obeyed.

They marched me back to my cell, which had once again been cleaned, and to my surprise, I found myself falling asleep. As I passed over, I realized that my exhaustion was not the product of tiredness, but whatever they had shot into my arm.

As I slept I dreamed. At first they were swirling, colored dreams, full of fields and fresh air, cool water and breezes. That was probably my mind wishing for something besides the stifling heat of my cell. But as they went on they changed. I was in the room with the wooden table again, being whipped. But now the lashes felt good, and each time the black leather belt landed across my ass or my back I felt waves of lust shoot through my cock. All the whip meant to me now was sex. I found myself wanting more and more. Whoever was whipping me stopped, and I started begging for them to whip me again. There was cruel laughter, and the whipping started again, and I reveled in it!

Again the whipping stopped, and again I begged; but this time my begging was useless. They wanted me to beg for something else. They would only whip if I would do other things for them. I begged to know what they wanted, and they told me it was my mouth they wanted and my ass. I told them to take me, to fuck my mouth and my ass as much and as long as they wanted; only please, whip me some more!

I felt something shoved up my ass and it nearly tore me apart. I felt and tasted a cock shoved into my mouth, but I couldn't see whose it was, and it didn't matter. I twisted and writhed as the cock in my ass and the one in my mouth began fucking me from both ends.

Then the whip landed on my back and the pain in my asshole, the choking in my throat, didn't matter. I felt my cock hard against the wood of the table, and the exquisite pain of the whip, and I was so happy — no, not just happy, sublimely ecstatic. I felt I would die from the sheer pleasure of it. That I would explode with the building waves that racked me.

Then the sergeant's face swam up before me in the darkness, and he smiled, and he said: "Come!" — And the explosion hit, flooding out of my cock like a river bursting a dam!

But even as the orgasm hit, I was back in the fields of light and cool water.

I was in pastures that seemed to stretch forever. I knew that I could run as far as I wanted to, and that no one would pursue me. I knew that I was totally free!

But I also felt intensely aware of the fact that my cock was suddenly soft, that the orgasm had passed, and that there was nothing in those wide pastures to turn me on.

Abruptly I was back in the room with the wooden table again, and once more I was begging to be whipped; and then the whole sequence repeated itself! The begging, the whipping, the fucking and the sucking. I felt my orgasms build, I saw the sergeant's face, and I came on cue, crying out with the pleasure of it.

But this time my return to the Elysian Fields was not so sudden. After I had come, I felt myself dragged roughly up from the table, carried to a window, and hurled out. Fear took hold of me as I fell, and I felt myself almost jarred awake. In that second I was aware that the sergeant was really there, standing over me as I slept, speaking softly to me. Then I saw rocks shooting up at me, and I felt my body broken as I crashed down on them.

Then I was in the fields, amid the cool streams. I realized that this place of pleasure and freedom was a kind of heaven, and that to get to it I had to die, not only in my body, but in my desires. If I wanted the freedom of the Elysian Fields, I had to give up the pleasures of the flesh. I had to give up the joy of being whipped and fucked and sucked. Of being allowed to worship my sergeant's cock and balls and living the life he wanted me to live.

I found myself whimpering and crying, huddled down in the middle of a huge meadow, begging to be taken back to the room with the wooden table.

And my wish was granted.

I was back there, and they were whipping me again, and all I wanted was to be there forever.

But I wasn't allowed that. The dream repeated itself again, and when the sergeant said "Come!" I came, and then I was thrown out on the rocks to die, and this time it was more intense and more real.

I don't know how many times the dream repeated, each time becoming more intense and more real. I dreaded the moment of being hurled out into space, of being broken on the rocks, of awakening in heaven. But I dreaded more the thought of not achieving that all-powerful orgasm at the sergeant's command. All creation seemed to revolve around that sublime moment, and it was all creation that I wanted.

How long I lay in my drug-induced stupor, the sergeant pouring ideas and desires directly into my subconscious, I don't know. When I finally awoke, my body ached all over, and my mouth tasted as if I'd chewed the sweat out of every Marine jockstrap that had ever been worn. I was dripping with sweat and my head ached, and I was vaguely hungry.

My bowels moved; I washed my face with water from the tap; and I sat down on my rack with my head in my hands. I wondered if I would feel pleasure the next time they whipped me; for I remembered my dreams quite clearly, and had an impression that if I tried hard I could remember more than the dreams. There had been someone in the room besides the sergeant; that much I knew, and they had conversed. Maybe if I could remember what they had said, I could counteract it.

But to what purpose?

It was definitely in my own interest to let this mass of suggestion take effect. However my body might be responding, I did not perceive the whippings as pleasurable! If what the sergeant had done would make them feel good, then I could always see a psychiatrist later. At least I would survive.

My guards came for me a little while later, and the sergeant gave me two pills and told me to take them. I did so, and they marched me out.

The scalding shower didn't exactly feel good; but the heat of it relaxed my muscles, and by the time we were marching down the hall, me with my hard-on, my head had stopped hurting and cleared.

We took a new route and moved through areas that looked newer than the ones I'd been in before. The walls were painted white, and the doors were painted shiny black, with only a minimum of scuffs along the baseboards. It even smelled newer.

The redhead opened a door and I was ushered into a room that nearly sent me into shock.

To begin with, the room was all mirrors. The walls, the ceiling, even the floor under a thick plastic coating — all were covered with mirrors. It was unnerving to see everything, including myself, reflected and reflected.

What was more unnerving was that the room was full of men.

In groups, just like the one of which I was a part, the room was filled with men. Near one wall three Marines watched over a naked man doing push-ups. Near another wall three Marines oversaw a naked man working with weights. In all there were at least ten groups, each one centered on a naked prisoner, each prisoner doing some kind of heavy exercise, each one sweating with the strain of it.

"Here," said my sergeant. "Look at this!"

I turned and he pointed to my image in the mirror, and that was the biggest shock of all.

I had been pleased with my body, and thought it not unattractive. I remembered looking in the mirror after I took that last shower on board ship before going up to the Old Man's office. What was before me now was a parody of what I had been that day.

My blond hair was shaggy and unkempt, and I had a beard! Somehow it had not occurred to me that I was going without shaving every day and that a beard does grow in. The shame of having my body hair shaved off had made me forget my facial hair.

True, it wasn't much of a beard. If it had been, I would probably have got a charge out of discovering it was there. But as it was, I wasn't old enough yet for it to grow thick, so it was sparse and dark blond, with a touch of red, and it just looked ratty.

The hair on my chest and around my cock and balls was coming back, too. But it was still short, and there was no nice mat on my chest, or bush around my balls. That made what had happened to my body all the worse.

I had always had a 'swimmer's body.' Thickly muscled, but with none of the muscles bulging. Now the tone of the muscles was gone. I hadn't kept up my calisthenics in my cell, and it hadn't taken long for everything to go soft. Worse, the food they'd been giving me had made me go flabby. And the lack of sunlight left me pale and pasty. Looking in the mirror, all I could think of was some kind of drug-wasted hippie. Even my blue eyes seemed dull and lusterless. I think I wept.

"Now," the sergeant said, obviously satisfied with my reaction, "Come and look at this!"

He led me to the center of the room and my humiliation was complete. There before me stood a man as beautiful as any I have ever seen; or so it seemed at that moment. His was much the same type of build that mine had been, but a little more so in all directions. His hair was curly and blond; his eyes were blue and flashing bright. His torso was muscled like a swimmer's, but the definition of the muscles was much clearer. He had the same kind of curly mat of hair on his chest that I had possessed, the same curly bush around his genitals. His waist was slim, his stomach a true 'washboard.' His legs were powerful and his cock and his balls bigger than mine. His cock was hard as a rock, and he was impaled on a rod that stuck up from the floor, swelling to a larger size and covered with a flesh-colored plastic phallus, where it vanished up his ass.

"This is Fido," said the sergeant. "That rod up his ass has a dildo mounted on the end, and it sticks way up in him. He can't go anywhere because he can't get himself up off it. It's got a vibrator built into it, so his prostate is constantly being massaged; and that means his cock stays hard, waiting for someone to suck it. Don't you agree that Fido is in every way superior to you, scum?"

It was said so pleasantly that when he called me 'scum,' it was as if he'd called me by my Christian name in the most friendly and cheerful manner.

"Yes, Sir!" I said, but with practically no force behind it. It was so self-evident, I felt, that it didn't require much agreement from me.

"You'd like to be able to do something for someone as beautiful as Fido, wouldn't you, scum?"

"Sir! Yes, Sir!" I said.

"Well, good!" said the sergeant heartily. "You can see that standing there all day with that thing up his ass is hard work. You can see how the heat bothers him from the way he's sweating! Wouldn't you like to take his place? Have that dildo up your ass instead?"

"Sir! Yes, Sir!" I said, gulping. I didn't know how big the dildo was, but

I really didn't want to find out.

"Well, good!" said the sergeant. "Maybe someday we'll give you that privilege! For now, you can help Fido by cooling him off. Get down and start licking the sweat off him. From the feet up. Don't suck him off though unless I tell you to. And if I do, it will only be after he's clean. Understand?"

"Sir! Yes, Sir!" I said.

I got down on my knees and looked up briefly at Fido. From where I knelt, he looked like a god, his powerful body standing over me, his slightly spread legs like columns; his great hard cock like the boom of a crane reaching out above me.

I bent down and started to lick his feet. They were beautiful feet, wonderfully formed, with high arches and perfectly shaped toes. The toenails were clean and neatly trimmed as if he'd been groomed by a beauty salon. It occurred to me to think that he was like a prize dog indeed, carefully prepared for a show by his master and standing in just the pose required for the judging.

The sweat on his feet had run down the whole length of his body, so it was strongly salty. The flesh that I licked seemed curiously cool, considering how much he was sweating; but then, feet are often colder than the rest of the body. I tried to lick under his arches, but then I realized that, impaled as he was, he couldn't lift either foot for me very readily. Still, as I started to move away from them and go up his ankles, he raised himself on his tiptoes. I didn't know whether he really wanted his arches licked or whether he was trying to respond to me. I dutifully got down on the floor on my stomach and started to lick his arches and the soles of his feet, looking up as I did so to his ass, where part of the dildo had slid downward.

It was much larger than the billy club they'd used on me, and I was glad the sergeant had postponed my session of relief for Fido.

When I finished with his heels and moved back up to his ankles, he lowered himself again and the dildo slid in up to the hilt. I heard him sigh almost silently, and wondered just how far it went.

I licked his strong, thick calves, realizing that I was thirsty with all the heat, and that his sweat, though salty, was helping. I went up his powerful thighs, admiring the sheer strength of them, and then I was at his balls, with his heavy, hard cock touching my head, then my face. By now I was excited, and though I knew it might earn me some harsh punishment, I took every opportunity to let my hard cock brush against Fido's legs.

I licked his heavy, hairy balls, and felt them fall wetly against my face. The musky smell of his balls, the hard length of his shaft on my forehead and in my hair drove me to a frenzy. I thought about the black-haired sailor in the movie, licking the Marine's balls. I thought about Fido's big cock shooting hot come all over my face. I started licking up the shaft of his cock, all reason running out of me like water out of a paper bag. I started to take the purple head of it into my mouth.

I felt the sergeant's hand on my shoulder, and I drew back, gasping.

"Get around back!" the sergeant ordered.

I moved around in back of Fido and started licking up the backs of his thighs. I got to his butt and felt him squirm on the big dildo and I licked over each buttock, then down the crack of his ass. He tried to twist so that my tongue would reach his asshole, but the dildo took care of that. The best I could do was lick to the point where the dildo entered, then down between his legs, to the base of his balls.

I wanted to lick his balls again, to suck them, to go on to his cock. He was writhing down, twisting with the pleasure of what I was doing, responding to the vibrator deep inside him. I saw him knot his fists, desperately resisting the urge to grab his cock and start jacking. I knew that if he did that, some terrible punishment must be in store for him, and I felt my heart go out in sympathy to him. If only I could help him out!

But the only thing I could do was keep myself under control, do what I was ordered to do; and if I was lucky, and Fido was lucky, maybe they'd let me get him off in the end.

I moved up, licking over his ass again lightly, tasting the salty sweat, then went to work on the base of his spine, and that little tender spot at the bottom of the small of the back. If there is anything as erotic as the genitals and the nipples, it has to be the spine. The very thought of a hot tongue licking its way up the spine is enough to excite most people. When it's actually happening to you, it's incredible.

I licked his spine, his wide, muscular shoulders, and then the sides of his back. All he could do to control himself now was lock his hands behind his back. I continued licking, but I didn't waste the opportunity to brush my cock against his ass and as I began on the back of his neck, against his gripped hands. It seemed to me that it might be a way of communicating with him, of letting him know . . .

Of letting him know what? That I desired him? Hell, I was leaving him no doubts about that as my tongue went into his ears, licking around in every little curve and crevice. I was on my tiptoes now, so that I could reach his ears without his having to lean back; and my cock was pressed right against his clasped hands. Suddenly I felt his hands unclasp and one of them seize my cock. I went wild and plunged my tongue deep into his ears, licking furiously as he squeezed and pulled hard at my member.

"Bad dog, Fido!" said my sergeant, sliding his arm deftly between us and pulling us apart. "You'll spend a week in the kennels for that!"

Fido groaned in anguish, and the sergeant drew me around in front of him.

"Now clean his belly!" the sergeant said.

I started licking hungrily up his perfect washboard stomach, but now the lust was unbearable because his hard cock was right against my chest. I licked up his belly, his chest, his sides, devoting extra attention to his tits, which now seemed to me as wonderful as anything in the world. I licked their pink softness until they grew rough and hard, then I ran my tongue over them some more, tickling them and making Fido whimper with pleasure.

Although I wanted to fuck him, although I wanted him to fuck me, although I wanted everything about Fido, I found that I was beginning to enjoy his writhing at my ministrations. There was a certain pleasure to being able to control somebody else's body. To give them a pleasure they could not endure, and have them respond at your very whim. I thought with complete contempt of the times I'd fucked girls and of the delight I'd got by bringing them to orgasm. That had been no more than a minor effort of self-control. All I had to do was keep pumping away, keep from coming, and they would eventually go off. But this, this bringing Fido to the edge and keeping him there, making him whatever I wanted — even as the sergeant made me whatever he wanted — this was something far more exciting!

I licked up his chest, then up his throat. Then I started licking his face. His mouth opened and his tongue came out, trying to meet mine, but I refused to kiss him. I licked over his tongue, I licked over his lips, but then I licked his nose, and his eyelids, his brow, his cheeks, and again, his ears.

By then he was moaning "Please, *Please!*" over and over, and I was right up against him, my cock pressed up hard against his belly, his hard cock between my legs, rubbing against my balls. I knew that if the sergeant told me to, I could come with no effort. I wondered if it would be all right to raise my hands and take his handsome head in my hands, and even kiss him. But the way he kept his hands down, and what I'd been taught, prevented me.

I was about to lose my control once again when the sergeant told me to stop and back off. I did as I was told, delivering one last tiny lick to his tongue, then standing back, stimulated beyond my wildest imaginings. Was this what the sergeant had put into my subconscious during the night? If so, I liked it!

"Fido's been bad," the sergeant said after a moment. "He's gonna have to spend some time in the kennels. But you've done very well, Rover, so I'm going to give you a treat. I'm gonna let you suck Fido off. Would you like that?"

"Sir! Yes, Sir!" I said, delighted. I also remembered that he had called me 'Rover' once before, and somehow it gave me a sublime pleasure. It was the only time I had been called by any proper name since I'd come to the Brig.

"Get down there and do it," the sergeant smiled.

I got down on my knees and took Fido's big cock right into my mouth. I sucked on it, I ran my tongue over it, I pulled it in and out. I heard him moaning and looked up at him as I sucked, his beautiful face a mask of ecstasy. I sucked harder, tasting the salt of his sweat, and now the saltiness of his pre-come oozing out of his cock and into my mouth. I pushed my tongue into the slit at the end, licked at the tender area under the head, slid it with a rush deep down my throat.

It didn't take long. I didn't know what else might have happened to Fido before I entered the room, but what I had done was enough. With a shriek his iron hardened even more and the cream gushed out into my mouth, soapy and sweet and tingling alive as it came. I sucked harder and he grabbed my head, trying to pull me off. I had the advantage though, because he couldn't move, being impaled, and I held on, sucking him harder and harder as he came. He started yelling and thrashing and pulled at my hair, and still he came, filling my mouth as fast as I could swallow. Then, abruptly, the taste of his come changed, and I realized that I had taken him past his threshold, and he was pissing, there being no more come in him.

I pulled my mouth away, and a spurt of yellow shot into my face.

The sergeant laughed.

"You liked getting him there," he said. "Now finish your job!"

I took Fido's cock back in my mouth, sucked again, and he pissed some more. Finally that too stopped, and I was allowed to pull back, my own cock harder than stone, and my body pouring sweat.

Fido was finally exhausted. He stood, his knees shaking, and I'm sure he would have fallen right then and there had it not been for the rod that held the dildo up his ass, impaling him.

My sergeant nodded to another sergeant across the room, and the other sergeant started across the room, apparently to do something about Fido. I wasn't allowed to see what, however, because I was drawn to my feet by the redhead and ushered out through a door opposite the one I'd come in by, a door also covered in mirrors, like the rest of the room.

The sergeant and the dark corporal had stayed with Fido, I supposed to explain something to this keeper. When the door closed behind us, I was alone with the red-haired corporal in a sort of corridor. The redhead smiled that cruel smile of his and reached out to play with my hard cock.

He masturbated me for a couple of minutes, not hard enough to bring me off, but enough to make me feel it coming. Then he worked on my tits for a while, using his fingernails to bite and twist them. If I had been in ecstasy before, I was doubly so now.

The door opened and the sergeant and the dark corporal came into the corridor, closing it behind them. The sergeant passed by me, not even looking at me, and walked down the corridor to inspect some curious installations in the wall. The redhead stopped playing with me, and I was able to watch what the sergeant was doing, and see the installations.

The corridor was lined with white tile and dimly lit with fluorescents. In one wall there was a series of holes, each with a little sliding door at the top, each with a basin a couple of feet below it. In one or two of the basins there was piss dripping, I could see, from the hole. On the ones with piss in them, the sergeant slid the little door down, closing off the hole.

"Ever hear of African roulette?" the redhead grinned at me.

"Sir! No, Sir!" I said.

"You have a board fence, see?" he said. "And there are six knotholes. Behind five of them are cocksuckers, and behind the sixth one is a cannibal!"

He laughed uproariously at his joke, and the other two Marines smiled, whether at him or the joke I couldn't tell.

"Come here!" the sergeant commanded.

I did as I was told.

"This is the latrine," he said. "Stick your dick in it!"

I moved up and stuck my dick through the hole he'd indicated, and immediately there was a mouth on the other side sucking it in.

"Fuck it!" the sergeant said, and with overwhelming enthusiasm I did just as he said.

I had no idea who was on the other side of the wall, but whoever it was was one hell of a cocksucker! He did everything I'd done to Fido, and a lot more. I hunched my ass back and forth with a violence I'd never even thought of with a woman, fucking his mouth so hard I thought sure I'd choke him. But he kept on, and it wasn't long before I came, shooting the whole load rapidly down his throat and pressing my body up against the white tile wall so that I could get my cock in as far as possible.

When I finished I started to pull back, but the sergeant's hand pushed against my ass, and kept my dick through the hole in the wall.

"Don't you have to piss?" he asked.

I realized that I did. And slowly, as my cock softened, I let the warm

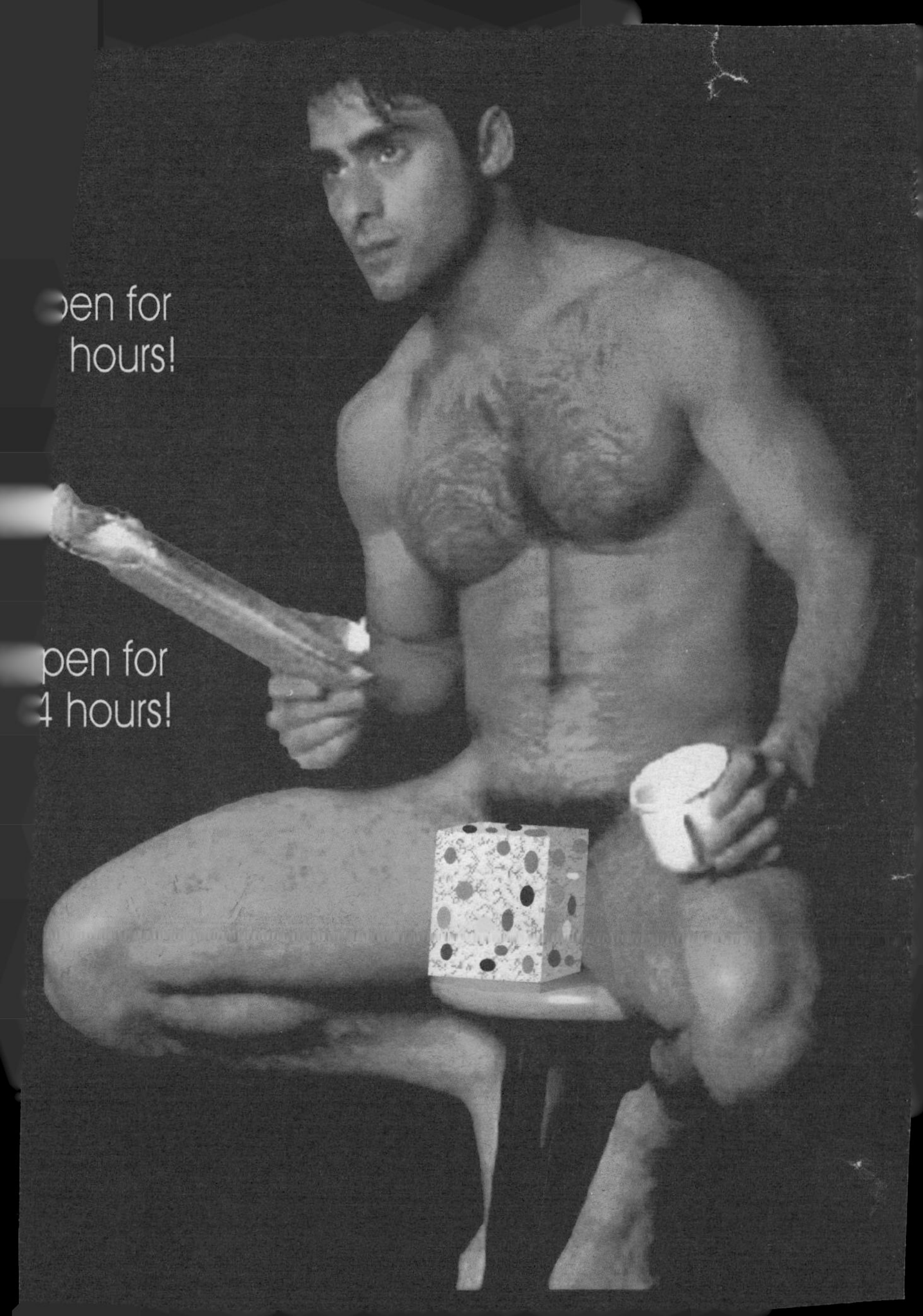

EVERY SUNDAY

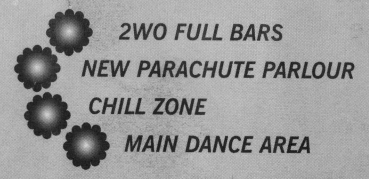

2WO FULL BARS

NEW PARACHUTE PARLOUR

CHILL ZONE

MAIN DANCE AREA

THE PROMISE IS TO PROVIDE MUSICAL FREEDO[M]
CAMP CLUBBING BEYOND THE VERNACULAR, HIGH END INTEL[L]
MASSIVE SOUND REINFORCEMENT AND LUMINESCENT P[

the kitchen. essex street, temple bar, [

admission £5. 11pm - tres late

EYE[

Disp[e

Opti[

DUCKie

We have just been sent their new line up for the forthcoming months.

installing 10k sound systems in 2 rooms. There are 2 arches of sound : new medikation with progressive trance and pumping techno and medikation groove featuring funky house and disco.

It all starts at 4.30am on monday 14th through til very late (usually about mid afternoon)

The Drome is 2 minutes from London bridge station (its literally underneath it, off Tooley street) with parking in the club from 6am.

If you're a shallow, Greek, Grandiurpass you may be considering having a nose job. After all its very common and counts as rather minor plastic surgery. 6,800 were performed last year in the U.K. alone. However there are certain things that you should know but you will not be told.

First of all, your consultant will not mention that it is very fucking painful. I am not a totally naive idiot, I did not imagine myself awaking in a scented private room filled with flowers, the surgeon beside me removes my bandages to reveal a sleek perfect nose, he passes me a mirror and tells me everything went smoothly but he'll write me a note allowing me two weeks leave from my well paid job to give me time to readjust to my enhanced beauty.

A drama queen I may well be but the actual experience was very, very, very far removed from this fluffy fantasy.

Wheeled back into the ward I am left with blood gushing from my nose for hours, unable to breath through my nose for two weeks because it would be blocked up with crusted blood and mucous and if you try to blow your nose you can upset the setting of the cartilage and change the shape permanently. Breathing only through your mouth dries the tongue until you can hear it scrape against the walls of your cheeks. Two weeks of sleeping sitting upright to prevent swelling. Oh yes did I mention the swelling?

Human bodies react to being chiselled, stitched and sliced, which results in two black eyes, blotchy skin and an enormous great big round hooter like a claymation character. The added joy of the bruising and inflammation is that after the initial horror of seeing the immediate results, you are left in suspense for two weeks waiting to discover what you will look like and whether this has been the most expensive fuck up of your entire life. If you are vain (oh the irony) you will not want to horrify your lover by making them see your gaping bloody face around the house even if it's on the premise of enhanced sexiness in the future. So if you're going to do this you may want to make sure you're single. the celibacy fits in just fine with the rest of your misery.

So, that was my experience of a nose job. Obviously now three weeks

beautiful, rich friends shower me with at every opportunity and of course infinite successes at everything i choose to do. But can you imagine all that yourselves. Just remember, next time you glimpse a daddy's girl or boy with suspiciously angular features floating along in life, remember that the cost isn't just financial. the real price is the cost to your dignity by the process. the pain, the paper underwear, the month of snoring and ask yourself, do you have the depth of personality to under

The Most popular types

RHINOPLASTY - nose job
SMALLDICKHOTOMY - pen...
FELLOVER WHILE HOOVE...
from anus
LOBOTOMY - mental surge...
LARDASSOTOMY - gets yo...
TRACHEOTOMY - essentia...
ENDOSCOPY - prepares yo...
COLONOSCOPY - what yo...
CARDIAC ARREST - the la...

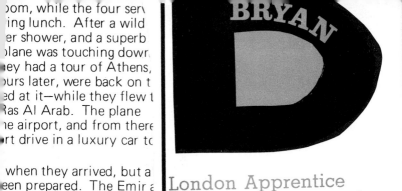

BRYAN D

oom, while the four ser
ing lunch. After a wild
er shower, and a superb
plane was touching dowr
ey had a tour of Athens,
ours later, were back on t
ed at it—while they flew t
Ras Al Arab. The plane
ne airport, and from there
rt drive in a luxury car tc

when they arrived, but a
een prepared. The Emira
together, and then the
one of his servants to
am to his room. Graham
e cottoned on that some-
t quite right when the
accompanied by two
ds. But he blew a kiss to
nd followed the servant,
rds falling in behind.
ought, as he said, it was
ce security, and nothing
r.

along a corridor and
to a different wing of th
a winding staircase, and
vast hall—that had a
tiful blond men sitting
o were watching an
lm on the TV-Video,
aying chess, the others
or lounging around
vo or three looked up
ne in.

t minute, Graham was
One of the guys nearest
American twang:
ock-sucker. Hi there
me to the hareem!''
ened in amazement, and
icion. The American
came over to him. He laic
and on Graham's shoulde

London Apprentice

It hardly seems a year since the London
Apprentice opened its doors to the gay
masses. MSC London, of course, had been
using the bar for a couple of months before.
The pub was one of the very few in London
to have a twelve o'clock licence and this did
help to at tract people to the unexplored
regions of the East End. But now even
better news—the LA has now got a two
o'clock licence! SO, on Tuesdays, Fridays
and Saturdays you can drink all the way
through till 2am; plus the fact that on
Sundays, at lunchtime, they will be open
from one till three, and in the evening they
will be open from eight till eleven thirty!
It's going to be very interesting to see how
clubs like the Cellar and Subway react! At
the present moment I can't see many
people forking out an entrance fee when
they can drink till two at pub prices!
Many congratulations to Michael and his
staff.

Expectations

Keeping my fingers crossed, and everything else for that matter, it seems that
gay guys may have found another ghetto
far away from Earl's Court. Apart from
the LA, a new restaurant and a leather and
rubber shop have opened in Hoxton Square.
The shop is called 'Expectations' and is
found at number 56. It opens Mondays to
Thursdays from 11am to 6pm, and on
Fridays and Saturdays from 11am to 10.30.
Jimmie Caffrey and I popped over the
other day, on a very crisp November morn-

stream of it flow out through my sensitive prick and into the invisible mouth that waited, holding it warmly, licking it. It was a kind of pleasure I had not even dreamed existed.

I wondered if the Roman emperors had conceived of the luxury of a mouth to piss in.

Nine

We left the corridor with the latrine by a different door than the one we'd entered through and marched down more corridors. Eventually we ended up back at the showers, and once again I was scalded clean. From there, my cock hard once again after the sergeant's fiddling with it, we went to the Room with the Wooden Table.

My schedule so far had called for one major item of torture or humiliation per day. Now I perceived that they were going to up the schedule. I remembered the dreams the sergeant had put into my mind and wondered whether or not they would actually throw me through a window. But as there were no windows, and as I'd clearly been killed on the rocks in my dream, I figured that part unlikely; at least, I hoped it was unlikely!

Much to my surprise, my three guards ignored me for a few moments. It was as if I was now somehow beneath their notice. Instead of watching me, they devoted themselves to stripping and hanging their clothes up neatly on pegs that I hadn't noticed before.

If the sight of their bare chests and cocks had been exciting, the sight of the three of them standing naked and sweating in the heat of the room was almost too much to stand. I was overwhelmed by the sheer beauty of their maleness, overpowered by the masculine smell of their sweat. I knew that something remarkable must be coming, because this was the first time I'd seen any of them fully naked.

They put their boots back on, without the socks, and that established quite clearly the relationship that was between us. However naked they might be, they were not vulnerable.

The dark corporal picked up some rope off the floor, something that I knew was not there before, and gestured to me to get up on the Table.

Was he going to whip me with the rope? I wondered as I climbed up and lay face down.

No. The sergeant and the redhead pulled me by the shoulders so that my head was off the end of the table. It twisted my cock painfully under me, but

I knew they'd be pleased by that.

They took my arms over the sides of the table and stretched them down toward the floor, then wrapped the rope round and round them so that they were bound securely to the legs of the table, but not tightly. I couldn't move, but my circulation was not cut off either.

"You're first!" I heard the sergeant say, and the redhead came and stood before me, his long, thin pecker, with its large, purple head, hard as a rock before my face, the foreskin stretched back and taut.

"I told you," said the redhead, smiling, "that you were gonna get to suck it, now didn't I?"

"Sir! Yes, Sir!" I said.

And then I felt the first lash across my back.

"The trick is," said the redhead, "to suck it without any biting. That's gonna be hard, with them whipping you, ain't it?"

"Sir! Yes, Sir!" I responded, and another lash landed from the other side. I realized with terror that I was to have two men whipping me now! And I knew that if I flinched and hurt the man whose cock I was about to suck, they'd have something dreadful to do to me.

"Well, now you know the rules of the game," I heard the sergeant laugh behind me, "you might as well start playing!"

Another lash landed on my back, and at the same moment, one across my ass, a harsh, brutal lash ten times more powerful: I knew that the dark corporal was in action.

I lifted my head and opened my mouth, realizing that the strain on my neck muscles was going to be as bad as the whipping before I was finished. The redhead stepped forward and slid his cock into my mouth, and two lashes, one after another, landed across my ass.

He started to fuck my mouth slowly, sliding the long tool in and out at a leisurely pace. I tried to suck the way I had sucked Fido's cock, with enthusiasm, but it was hard to do because of the belts landing hard on my ass. I wished my hands were free, so that I could support my neck and head, but it was hopeless. What I had come to think of as an ultimate reward and pleasure, the final opportunity to suck off the men who'd been whipping me, was becoming an even worse torture.

His cock was longer than I'd thought from previous glimpses, and as he picked up speed, it choked me, going deeper and deeper down my throat each time. I tried to relax my throat and let it go, the way you have to relax your throat when the doctor tells you to say 'Ah!' But it was all I could do to keep from biting him as the belt landed again and again.

With part of my mind I realized that they were concentrating on my ass now totally. They weren't whipping my back at all, just the cheeks of my ass, and that hard as hell. I felt it glow red as my body involuntarily struggled, my cock working against the wood of the table. I was afraid that I might do something wrong, but there was no part of me left to monitor all my actions at once. My prick was hard, twitching against the wood every time a blow landed on my ass. My legs thrashed against the pain, helpless because of my bound arms. My neck ached and my mouth and throat were being violated more and more harshly as the redhead fucked faster and faster, deeper and deeper. I was afraid I was going to gag. What would they do to me if I puked on him?

Suddenly the blows started falling twice as fast, no pause between them, and the redhead rammed his cock all the way down my throat. I screamed, or tired to, and felt white-hot come pouring into my throat. His cock pulsed against my tongue, and I could feel the waves of semen flooding through it, even before they gushed out.

And then it was over.

The whipping stopped, the redhead pulled his long, partially hard prick out of my mouth, told me to lick the last of the come off it, and then it was the sergeant's turn.

There were tears running down my face and that seemed to please him. He wiped them off with his fingers and licked them, smiling. Then he stood up and lifted my head and slid his thick, dark cock into my mouth.

I tried to look up at him, up past the hairy expanse of his belly and his thickly muscled chest. By rolling my eyes all the way up, I could see him smiling down at me. He stroked the side of my face like a father touching a daughter's face. He seemed the very model of gentleness and kindness at that moment. His thick, big tool filled my mouth completely, and the musky smell of his crotch was overpowering right against my face.

I saw his white teeth shine through his lips as his smile grew slightly. Then he nodded and I felt the two belts land hard on my ass.

It had been possible to keep my teeth away from the redhead's cock because he was built long and thin. But the sergeant was not only long, he was thick. I found myself scraping him more and more as he fucked away at my mouth. I didn't want to hurt him, not only because of the punishment he would mete out, but simply because I wanted to give him as much pleasure as possible. I found that I was failing increasingly as he fucked, because not only was he thick, he was rough.

The redhead had started slow and built up to a faster rhythm. The sergeant just started fucking at full speed, and after a moment grabbed hold of my head to steady it. There wasn't much time to think about what was happening to me now: I was just an object, one helpless before the onslaught of forces too great for it. He fucked and they whipped, and I moaned and writhed, and that was all there was to existence. His black, crinkly pubic hairs rammed against my face, his big, pendulous balls slapped against my chin, and he fucked my face as if that was all it had ever been designed for.

Then, with a rush and a monstrous male groan, he came. He didn't shove it all the way in, the way the redhead had, but kept on fucking as wave after wave of sweet, soapy come shot into my mouth. I tried to lick the head of his cock to give him more pleasure; but he was still fucking too fast and I only succeeded in getting my tongue rammed back against my palate.

Finally, my sergeant, too, was finished.

I knew what was coming next, and the very thought of it scared me. I remembered the pleasure with which the dark corporal had filled my mouth with asparagus piss, the delight he'd taken in putting those alligator clips on my tits. And I remembered that his cock had filled my mouth even soft. I didn't know how I was supposed to get the thing in when it was hard!

But how I did it didn't concern the dark corporal, only that I did. I had thought it would be a relief to have him in front of me, rather than whipping me. At least some of the pain would go away, I thought. But I was wrong.

When he brought his smooth body before me I trembled, for his cock was even larger than I'd imagined, and I was sure there was no way for it to fit into my mouth. It was enormous, a huge, dark club, something more like a weapon than a prick.

He slapped it across my face a couple of times, to show me how hard and huge it was. Then he positioned it against my open mouth and shoved.

It was so big it hurt to have it in my mouth. My jaw ached with the effort of opening my mouth wide enough. I felt that if he put it even part way in, he would rip my mouth and throat apart.

But he knew what he was doing. He had done it many times before, and he knew just how to use his tool to get the job done. The whipping started and he began to fuck my mouth very gently, just a little bit of the huge plum head in and out.

"Lick it," he whispered, and I did as I was told.

My mind went numb, and eventually so did my aching jaws. Even my ass, with the belts wailing away at it, seemed to recede from reality. I noticed somewhere along the way that he was making longer and longer strokes with his giant organ; but it only surprised me. My mouth, and even my throat, seemed to be widening, expanding, so that I was taking more and more of his big, dark prick.

It was while the dark corporal was fucking my mouth that the changes started to take place in my perceptions. After the numbness a glow started, first in my buttocks, where the blows of the belts were landing, and then spreading through the rest of me. The pain started changing to a kind of pleasure, like the tingle one feels when icy cold hands are plunged in warm water. It hurts, but you would not take them out for anything! Or like the pins and needles you feel after your legs and arms have gone to sleep. You laugh at that kind of pain, and although you cringe from it, too, you don't move to stop it. The warmth of it floods through you, a different kind of pleasure. Only a little part of me realized that what was happening to me was the result of the sergeant's work on my dreams, the result of drugs.

My jaws hurt, but the pleasure of that big cock in my mouth, reaching deeper and deeper toward my throat, was more than ample reward. I could hardly wait for the gobs of come to pour out into my mouth. I felt as if the pleasure of the moment would surely bring me over the hill and I would come myself, shooting onto the wooden table, the semen gushing up between my belly and the wood.

The pain in my jaw became the same tingling pleasure as that in my glowing ass. It was all as good as a hot bath, as comfortable as a warm bed. The pain was transmuting into warmth and pleasure, and what in the world could be more wonderful?

The dark corporal slowed his fucking, then stopped, the big purple head of the cock resting right on my tongue, at the front of my mouth. He came, slowly, deliberately, as if it were something he'd learned in school.

Masses of white semen, what seemed like quarts of it, poured thickly out of his big prickhead and into my mouth. And it was vile.

Whatever he'd eaten this time, it made the asparagus piss taste good by comparison. It was bitter, and nasty, and words cannot describe it. It was like rotten clams, or decaying vegetation, or the worst medicine you ever had to take as a kid.

And it didn't shoot into my mouth, so that I could swallow it, it just poured slowly in huge quantities. And I *couldn't* swallow it, nor anything, because the head of his cock was so big, and my mouth so far open. I just had to let it fill my mouth, thick and viscous and filthy-tasting and alive

Finally, he withdrew and let me swallow it.

I thought I was going to choke on it, then I was sure I was going to puke it up again. But he was hoping for that, I knew, and he would have something worse ready for me. I fought down my urges and forced my mind to think about the burning of my ass, where I thought I must have taken many more than sixty lashes.

The dark corporal took his big, still-hard cock and rubbed it all over my face. It was still coated in semen, and I found I was glad he was doing it, rather than making me lick it clean the way the redhead had done.

But that, too, was a trap. When he'd coated my face with his come, he still made me lick it clean, and his big balls as well. This proved to be the worst kind of agony, because they had stopped whipping me, and most of the pain in my body seemed to be centered in the muscles at the back of my neck, the ones I'd used to hold my head up while sucking their cocks.

When the dark corporal finished with my mouth, they untied my arms and told me to get up. I did so, trying to slide off the table without having to sit on my ass. I was sure there must be blisters on it by now. They made me stand at parade rest for a few minutes, looking at the wall; then the redhead nodded his assent and I realized that my ordeal for the day was not going to be a two-parter, but at least three parts!

They moved me around to the foot of the table and had me stand up against it. The two corporals put their hands under my armpits and lifted me slightly, so that my cock and balls rested lightly on the table top. Then the sergeant wound the rope round and round my legs, binding them to the legs of the table in the same fashion that my arms had been previously bound: tight, firm, but not tight enough to cut off the circulation.

The corporals released my weight and I sagged in the ropes. My feet didn't touch the floor, so my weight was carried by the friction of the ropes around my legs. My balls were crushed up tight against my cock and my belly by the wooden table top.

"Lay down!" my sergeant smiled.

I bent forward and lay on the table top. My ass was now right off the end of the table, my legs spread apart, my cock and balls crushed beneath me. The two corporals took hold of my arms and stretched them toward the other end of the table, so hard that I felt as if I were being racked. While I was thus stretched , the sergeant produced some leather manacles, like the ones I'd seen in the training film, and fastened them about my wrists. Then he attached ropes to them and bound the ropes round the legs at the head of the table. I really was racked now, I thought, ropes and all!

There wasn't a muscle I could move, except my fingers and toes.

I felt the sergeant's hand sliding over my back, smoothing my skin, the way he sometimes did before a whipping. I felt his hand move down over the burning globes of my ass. He slapped my ass hard, and I grunted. That seemed to satisfy him.

"You're up, again!" he said.

The redhead came around and squatted down where he could look me in the face.

"I'm gonna give you all them things you wished for now," he said. "You remember. All them things you wanted to do? Well, you're gonna do them. This is your graduation, slave boy!"

I felt, more than saw, the sergeant and the dark corporal come to the sides of the table, about even with my hips. I felt, more than saw, the redhead go around to the foot of the table.

I felt him put the head of his long, thin, hard cock against my asshole.

And then I felt the two belts land across my back at the same moment he rammed his cock up my ass!

It wasn't gentle, the way the billy club had gone up. It was a savage, hard thrust, and I screamed for all I was worth. He didn't put it in a little at a time, he shoved the whole length of it.

If I had imagined that getting fucked would be somehow pleasurable, I was wrong. It hurt like hell, like nothing I had ever imagined. Maybe it wouldn't have if he hadn't wanted it to, but he did want it to, and it did. I kept screaming, and the whips landed again, and then the redhead started to fuck me in earnest.

When he'd put his cock in my mouth, he'd been careful of my teeth, and so he'd fucked carefully. Now there were no teeth to worry about, and he let himself go. He fucked hard, the way the sergeant had, and with no worries. He fucked savagely, ramming it in hard and deep, then ramming it in from different angles, battering at the sides of my insides until I was sure he'd tear me apart.

And all the while he fucked me, the dark corporal and the sergeant rained down blows on my back with their belts. There was nothing for me to do but scream, and so I did a lot of it. The way my arms were tied meant that new configurations of muscles were being whipped when I thought that I'd been whipped every way possible.

Eventually, as he fucked me, my asshole loosened up. The battering was still rough, but it began to become bearable. Then that mysterious change started to come over me, and the whipping on my back started to blend with what I was feeling up my ass, and the whole thing shifted to pleasure. It was still pain, but the suggestions the sergeant had planted deep in my mind were alive and working. As I felt the redhead go off, sending his hot fluids deep inside me where I'd never felt anything before, I too came.

My cock, crushed against the wood, burst forth with pulses of hot come, wet and warm against my belly, slippery on the wood, and painful in their violent discharge.

The whipping didn't stop. The redhead pulled out, came around to the side of the table, and took over for the sergeant. Then the sergeant went around to the back, I felt his big tool against my ass, and then it, bigger around than the redhead's, was pushing its way in.

The fact that a kind of pleasure had crept through me didn't stop me from screaming some more as he slowly shoved his cock deeper and deeper into me. I had loosened up enough to accommodate the redhead, but not enough to take the sergeant. It was like the whole thing starting over from scratch. His bigger cock was like doing it again for the first time.

Though he wasn't savage the way the redhead had been, the sergeant knew other ways to hurt. He rammed a little at a time, but always just a little deeper, and always just as the belts landed. My head was thrashing back and forth wildly by the time he was all the way in, and I was out of my mind. Nothing I had ever experienced was like having this big man's cock up my ass!

He started fucking, hard and fast. I went even wilder. I think if I'd been free to move I might have torn his tool right off, so much did I try to move my ass away from his onslaught. He fucked and fucked, and my throat grew raw from screaming before I felt him come deep in my ass, the sensation like alcohol being poured on an open cut. It was fire; it was pain; but it was a driving fulfillment of desire, too!

I barely noticed that I was coming as he pulled his cock out of my ass.

Then the whipping stopped and the full terror of what was about to happen hit me.

The pain of the whipping, I realized, had mitigated the pain of my rape. Now the whipping had stopped, and I looked up from the table to see the dark corporal standing where I could see him, sliding his fist back and forth around his huge, engorged penis: like a ramrod, a battering ram, a . . .

The sergeant's suggestions took hold.

"Please!" I started to babble. "Please, whip me some more! Please, *please whip me!*"

That was what he'd been waiting for. That was what he knew would be coming forth from me. That was what they'd all been waiting for.

The sergeant and the redhead walked slowly to the front of the table and laid down their belts, right in front of my face. The dark corporal walked around to the back of the table and positioned his cockhead at my asshole. I kept screaming and begging for them to whip me, knowing full well that whipping was what I wanted more than anything else in the world; knowing that whipping was always going to be better than any kind of sex: knowing for *absolute truth* any thing, any suggestion, any fantastic notion that would make bearable what was surely going to happen.

And then it happened.

I felt the big head probe at my ass. It was like a big animal nosing at the flap of your tent on a night in the wilds. It was like a giant monster looking into your window in a horror movie. Only it was real.

I felt it start to push in, to stretch my anus, wider and wider, past its previous stretching, wider, till I felt it start to tear. I kept screaming and begging for the whip, as I knew they wanted me to, and it kept coming in, wider and bigger and more awful.

And then I felt a light slippage, and I knew the head was in, intact.

It moved in, relentlessly, like a squadron of tanks, unstoppable. I felt my guts spreading out, stretched by the mass of it as it forged ahead. Nothing could stop it. It was like a tidal wave, huge and terrible, a force of nature.

It seemed to take forever for it to get all the way in. Time and again I was sure there couldn't be any more of it, or that there couldn't be any more room in me for it to fill. I knew it was only ten or twelve or thirteen inches long. That it couldn't be any more than that! But it seemed to take forever, to go on forever, and I found myself wondering crazily if it was going to come out of my mouth.

Then it was done, and I felt his groin, his pubic hair, up flat against my butt. I heard him sigh, and then I heard him laugh, a short, cold laugh. Then he started to fuck me.

He started slow. He had no need to be harsh or savage; the mere size of his weapon was enough to hurt me with every move. He drew all the way back, till his cock was almost out, then slid all the way in again. I felt a riptide in my guts as he did it, and then he did it again, a little faster. And then a little faster.

It was so complete a wrenching of my body — my ass, my intestines, sometimes I thought my stomach and my heart — that there wasn't room to think or after a while to feel. I didn't perceive the change in what he was doing for a long time, it coming to me very slowly that he was fucking me hard and fast and that my very bowels were now a thing to be controlled as sure as he controlled my tied and whipped and helpless body. They had owned my outside; they had got hold of my mind; and now, as the dark corporal fucked and fucked me, they even owned my bowels. I was theirs, inside and out, to do with as they willed.

He was like a huge machine. I saw images of the big guns on shipboard, their barrels pulling back and then shooting out as they fired. I saw images of the big, phallic shells the guns shot. I felt as if I were being shelled from the inside as he pumped his big prick into me over and over and with rising force.

I noticed that I had got hold of one of the belts with my teeth. That I was biting down on it. I also noticed that I wasn't screaming and begging anymore, only grunting in response to each of his gigantic thrusts.

The sergeant picked up the belt I wasn't biting and walked over to the back of the table.

"You still want to be whipped, Rover?" he asked.

"Sir! Yes, Sir!" I mumbled, not even aware of what I was saying.

And then I was shocked back into awareness of what was happening to me by a blow landing between my shoulder blades, a blow so hard I knew it could have only come from the dark corporal who was fucking me. And I heard him begin to cry out, even as I felt his huge weapon start to fire off inside me, even as he rammed harder and harder and started to land blow after blow across my back with the belt.

I was shocked by the suddenness of it, by the renewed intensity of the pain, by everything, and I bit down on the belt, and screamed hoarsely in my throat, and I came too. An angry, painful explosion out of my balls that fought to get through my cock and out onto the wooden table, fought to compete with the huge cock up my ass for my body's attention.

But my orgasm was nothing to me when compared to the monstrous orgasm the dark corporal was shooting off inside me, his huge organ tearing my ass and my guts apart with the violence of it, his powerful arms ripping the flesh off my back with the leather belt he was swinging!

I knew that I was going to die from what was happening to me, and I only wished it would be soon.

But I also knew that another part of me liked it.

Ten

When the dark corporal pulled his huge tool out of my ass, I felt like a balloon from which the air had all escaped. I couldn't imagine that he hadn't taken my guts with him. I hurt with waves of pain that I recognized to be in time with my heartbeat. The very blood that flowed through my veins was carrying the pain.

I didn't really notice it when they untied my legs and took the leather manacles off my wrists. I lay on the wooden table, my belly covered with my own come, trying to adjust my insides to their original shape. I was amazed that I had lived through it, but I was sure I wouldn't live for long.

I don't think there were any screams or tears left in me. They had all been whipped out. I don't think there was any part of me left that could feel pain anymore, either. What they hadn't assaulted had assaulted itself, writhing against the ropes, the table, or like my balls, expelling fluids in self-defense. My balls ached as if they had been whipped, too, but I knew it was just 'blue balls,' that pain you feel from too many, too frequent orgasms.

When I finally started to be aware of things again, the sergeant and the two corporals were all dressed. I wondered idly if they had left the room and taken a shower while I lay there, for certainly they looked refreshed and neat. It was hard to imagine that they had so recently been the animals who had ravaged my asshole and my mouth.

"Time to get up," the sergeant said when he saw that my eyes were focusing.

I didn't think I would ever get up.

"You'll find it easier than you think," he said, after a moment. "Besides, we're going to take you to a corpsman from here. Have to make sure you haven't been hurt, you know."

I wanted to laugh. The idea that I hadn't been hurt was the ultimate irony of the English language!

The sergeant didn't wait for me to respond. He lifted me gently, sliding his arm under my chest, and got me to a sitting position. From there I found myself wanting to stand, just so that I could get off my burning ass. I remembered that I had been tied to the table with my legs over the end. How I had come to be laying on the table completely I didn't know. I didn't think I had lost consciousness. But maybe I had, and there had been something so bad I couldn't even remember it!

They marched me down the hallways. Perhaps 'marched' is an exaggeration. They walked quietly and calmly, and I half-shambled, half-waddled. My ass was so sore I was sure I would never walk straight again.

It took forever, but they finally brought me to a door in the freshly-painted, new section of the building, the part with the white walls and the black doors. Only the sergeant entered with me, a fact that was vaguely disquieting, but only vaguely so; I hurt too much to be afraid.

Inside was a corpsman of some kind. He might have been a doctor, and looking back at it, I suppose he was a doctor as well as a torturer. He went over me with a lot of instruments, taking particular pleasure in examining my ass with a lot more fingers than any other doctor ever had.

Finally he made me stand in a shower stall, a white-tiled, very large one, and rolled over a metal stand with a big, black rubber enema bag hanging from it, above head level. He took the black plastic nozzle and slid it up my ass, then told me that he was going to fill me up, and that I was to hold it until he told me to release it.

He undid the fastening on the tube and I felt the warm water gush up into my insides, filling me until I felt as if I would burst. It tingled strangely inside me, and I wondered if there was something in the solution to ease my pain, or to increase it.

He made me do twenty deep knee bends, then lie down and do twenty sit-ups while the sergeant held my feet. If he'd made me do anything else, I know I couldn't have held it any more.

He opened a door, one of several along one wall, and told me to relieve myself in the toilet inside. I shambled in and sat on the tall, plastic cone that passed for a toilet in the little room, and let go. It wasn't so much a relief as an explosion, of the kind that you get when a night of drinking beer is topped by a case of the GI shits.

The sergeant stood watching me as I did it, smiling at me with satisfaction. When I finished I looked around for toilet paper, but there wasn't any.

"Don't worry," he said. "We're going to wash you off in the shower next. But first there's something I want you to see."

He came in and motioned me up from the toilet. I stood to one side, staring dumbly as he undid a catch on the floor, behind the toilet, and flipped the plastic cone forward.

Underneath where I had sat was a metal grillwork, all smeared with shit now, and under that was a pool of piss and shit, with a man in it. I had let fly all over his head, and the stench was awful.

The sergeant said nothing, but flipped the toilet back into place and fastened the catch.

I was dazed as he led me out into the medical room again, put me in the shower stall, and turned on the water.

I guess I expected to be scalded again, but I wasn't. It was a very warm, ordinary shower, and that made it all the scarier.

He tossed me a towel and I dried off, then followed his motion to come out of the shower. The corpsman handed him some kind of plastic cord device and he deftly moved my hands behind me, and with the plastic bonds, fastened them there.

I followed him across the room to one of the doors that lead to little, individual toilets. Inside he flipped the plastic cone forward and lifted the metal grillwork, this one clean and shiny. Below it was a small, porcelain tank, maybe four and a half feet deep. In one wall of the tank was a small, round hole, and in the bottom was a plug-like device, I presumed for draining the tank.

"Get in!" the sergeant smiled.

I squatted, sat on the floor, and slipped my feet and legs over the edge and into the tank. I remembered the other man, the one whose head I had shit on, and looked up at my sergeant, mutely imploring him, not daring to speak. He continued to smile, and his smile even brightened a little, probably because of the look he saw in my eyes.

"Get in," he repeated softly.

I slid off the edge and stood in the white porcelain pit.

"Turn around and face that little hole," he said.

I did so.

"Now get down on your knees."

I knelt, barely able to fit my body into the tight confines of the chamber. He lowered the grillwork and fastened it in place. My face was now directly in front of the little hole. I couldn't raise myself up any higher; but because it was so tight a fit, I couldn't fall over, either.

"You let your teeth get in the way," the sergeant said, "when you were sucking my cock. If you were a full-time slave, I'd just have your teeth all pulled, and then there wouldn't be any problem. But you're not. You're just a piece of Navy shit, a dog who needs training. So instead of pulling your teeth, I'm going to punish you, and let you get some practice at the same time."

He paused.

"You remember that little hole I let you stick your dick in this morning? Well, this is the other side of it. This is where the bad dogs have to do their duty. You really enjoyed having that slave suck you off this morning, so you'll be happy to know you're going to get to perform the same service for lots of other guys."

He paused again, letting it sink in, letting me wonder.

"The training is in two parts," he said after a few minutes as my knees began to ache where they rested on the porcelain. "The first part is the cocksucking and the piss-drinking. Anybody in the Brig can come down here and stick their dick in there, and anybody who does you suck. Lots of times it will just be for a piss, so you be sure and drink it all. Sometimes it will be with a hard-on, and you'd better damn well do a good job at it. If I get any bad reports, see, that's when I unlock the door up here, and they start using this toilet. So, you see, you've got a chance to avoid getting shit on if you're real good at sucking cock! And that's just what you want to learn to do real well, ain't it?"

It took me a moment to realize that he wanted an answer. Then I answered what he always wanted me to say: "Sir! Yes, Sir!"

"Well, good! You might turn out to be a pretty good slave yet, scum! You just keep sucking all those cocks, and keeping it first class, and this door may stay locked the whole time you're down there. — Oh, yeah! The time you're down is determined by how long it takes to fill up the tank you're in, see? You remember those little basins below the hole, don't you? Well, when the piss starts pouring out that little hole and filling up that basin, somebody will shut the little door and let me know you're done. By that time you'll be swimming in it up to your chin and will have processed a whole lot of piss!"

He must have heard the groan that escaped my lips.

"Now, don't you worry! Old Doc in there tells me that piss is sterile! It won't hurt you to drink it, unless you try drinking nothing else. Of course, that's just what you're going to be doing, but not for all that long, Rover. You'll probably be getting a little sick by the time we let you out, but don't worry, we're real experienced at dealing with this problem. You just put your trust in me, you hear?"

He waited for me to answer, and I said "Sir! Yes, Sir!"

"Well, good! Now you have fun down there!"

And with that he flipped the toilet up and locked it in place, and I was in darkness, except for the little hole in the wall, through which a small, cylindrical beam of dim white light shone.

I had time for all the pains in my body to congeal and become one enormous pain. To the welts on my back and ass, to the aching of my balls was added the agony in my knees and soon my arms, because they couldn't move. I wondered how long it would take for me to drink enough piss, and then piss it all out again, so that I was essentially floating in it. At least, I thought, once I was floating, my knees wouldn't hurt.

It wasn't long before the first cock appeared through the hole. I was so thirsty by then I fastened on it ravenously and started to suck. It responded quickly and got hard, no piss coming out, and I was sorry I hadn't just held it in my mouth, waiting for a drink. But whoever was out there was in a hurry and came quickly, and then he pissed, and my thirst was relieved.

It was much longer before I got my second drink; but that time I knew what to do, and he pissed before he got hard, and I had to suck him anyway.

There was one point when the room beyond the wall filled with men taking turns at the latrine, and I figured it must be a break in their day. I sucked ten or fifteen cocks at that point, but most of them wanted to piss. I began to worry if I could hold it all, and wondered what would happen if I couldn't. But I *knew* what would happen, I realized. The sergeant would unlock the door, and I would get shit on!

When I was so full that I couldn't hold any more, I figured out the answer. If I started in sucking hard the minute the cock got through the hole, they almost always got a quick hard-on, and then they had to wait to piss. That way I could buy extra time for my body to do its processing.

I wondered if someone would complain about being sucked when he didn't want it, but I realized that that was silly. If they didn't want any chance of being sucked, they would go to another kind of latrine.

The first time I pissed it was difficult to do. Like most people, my toilet training had been pretty thorough, and it was really very hard to just let go and do it. The feeling of the warm piss pooling around my knees almost stopped me, and I had to get set to do it all over again. Finally I got my bladder empty and relaxed as best I could in the moist atmosphere of my container, the smell of urine filling my nostrils in a way different from that when I drank it.

I tried counting the cocks I sucked, or noticing things about them, but that quickly got lost in the pain and humiliation of it all. There were some guys who were as big as the dark corporal and some who were rougher than the sergeant and some who must have avoided bathing for a week or two before they came on a visit to the latrine. I choked on one of those, but I guess that gave him a bigger thrill, because nobody came to unlock the upper door.

In the darkness and crampedness, in a period when there was nobody using me, I began to think back and look at the route that had brought me to this place. Along the path of my mental journey I came across the stories of the saints, in particular those around the time of the Renaissance who had got their sanctity by throwing themselves into the local 'black hole,' that pit of pestilence where the village idiot was wont to empty all the sewage that people tossed out of their windows into the streets each morning. It had been the absurdity of canonizing that kind of mortification of the flesh that had been one of the first things to turn me off the church.

Now, I thought, I was become an equal of a good many authentic saints. Not, perhaps, by intention, but certainly in a kind of martyrish way. I hadn't chosen my particular mortification of the flesh, but I had chosen to stick to my ethics and ended up here, just as a good many saints had done.

Another cock pushed through the hole, and I started sucking it, almost automatically now, my mind wandering. I think that was about the point that I started pissing and sucking both without thinking about it. I was just a part in a production line, and it wasn't necessary for my mind to be there for me to do my job. I had a whole life to think back on and if it took me away from my tortured body, that was what I wanted.

I figured out, though not consciously, that if I leaned forward a little, I could fall asleep with my mouth against the hole. The one thing that I was afraid of was that I might fall asleep and miss a cock, and get complained about. With my mouth against the hole, I would feel the thrust, open for it, and have the cock in my mouth before I was even awake.

I got very efficient at it.

I remember the point when the piss reached my balls, and then my ass, and how it started to sting a little. It struck me as odd that I hadn't shit myself, but then I remembered that I hadn't eaten anything really, and that what I had eaten must have come out with the enema.

I remember, too, the point when the piss reached my nipples. I sort of squirmed around, trying to make a little wave that would lap against them. That was the closest thing I could imagine to something that would feel good. Some time after that I realized that my head was swimming, that I was dizzy, and sick. But I was too far over the threshold into delirium by that time to understand what dizziness was.

It must have been shortly after that I became completely delirious, sucking all those cocks by habit and dreaming.

Eleven

I didn't have any shirt on and my arms were bound behind me. Not just at the wrists. My hands were clasping the opposite elbows, and a leather thong was wrapped around the forearms and wrists so that they were bound together. I was wearing some kind of tight-fitting things like stockings and over them something like a big pair of padded trunks. Inside these my cock and balls hung free as if the crotch had been cut out of a pair of long johns.

There was a guard to either side of me, and each wore elaborate suits of armor with fancy embossing all over the breastplate and helmets with plumes on them. They were not the ones who had brought me to the chamber; they were only the guards who took over from my captors.

The chamber was dark, but it smelled very good. I recognized the odor of sanctity; that peculiar blend of beeswax candles, incense, water, and hypocrisy. There were black velvet hangings all around the walls and two tripods with charcoal blazing in them to either side of a broad marble desk.

Behind the desk stood a figure in black, a tall figure made even taller by the peaked hood which covered his face. Only two eyeholes allowed him to see out through the hood, and I thought he looked like a grand something-or-other of the Ku Klux Klan, even though I couldn't quite remember what the Ku Klux Klan was. There was a symbol embroidered on his robe in scarlet, a cross that was clearly a sword turned upside down. He spoke; I recognized his voice, but couldn't place it.

"You have been accused of witchcraft," he said. "Witchcraft is a heresy, and the penalty for heresy is death. What have you to say for yourself?"

"I'm not guilty," I said. "I'm a true son of the Church and believe in the Lord as my Savior!"

"Yet you have committed an abomination before God, and we know this; for he whom you did it with has confessed everything. Do you deny that you were sodomized by the Viscount d'Esposa?"

My silence and panic gave him the assent he required.

"Sodomy is also punishable by death," he said at length. "But if you truly repent of it, your soul may yet be saved."

"Where is d'Esposa?" I asked, fearful for my lover's life and welfare.

"Where you might expect him. On the rack!"

My heart sank. The good, the beautiful Ramon, tortured because he had dared to love me! My heart broke, and I knew in that broken shell that God was not just or good, but a mocker, a deceiver, and evil! Worse, I knew that Ramon was beyond my help!

"I deny the charge!" I said vehemently. "I have done nothing wrong in the sight of God, neither sodomy nor witchcraft!"

"We shall see," said the Inquisitor. "Guards, bring him along!"

He opened the curtains behind his desk and they escorted me through a heavy wooden portal into a dark stone corridor. We walked down it, led by the Inquisitor, and began to descend a stairway. There were occasional candles on the walls, but there was very little light, and the air became oppressive as we descended, going down for what seemed like forever. I knew that I was beyond help now. No one could get into the citadel where the Inquisition kept its heretics imprisoned. How had I been so foolish as to assume there was any place where they did not have eyes?

I began to hear screams of agony echoing up from the pit below. My flesh crept with the terror of the place, a terror beyond any man's knowing; for indeed, no one had ever returned from this place alive, except on the way to the stake!

The smell from below was appalling, like the smell of a city after the visit of the plague. I wondered how many died here without the benefit of the flames.

We came to a level corridor with iron-barred doors to cells from some of which came groans of torment. We walked past all these, then descended another stairway. I wondered if the stairs of the citadel went down to Hell itself or if they merely brought up to earth the worst Hell had to offer.

They brought me to a great round chamber, vaulted and groined and lit by flickering red torches. Hideous shadows danced on the walls, and there was a constant music of anguished voices from diverse places around the walls, the chorus of the tortured and the damned.

The Inquisitor turned to face me, and I caught the glint of his dark eyes through the holes in his hood.

"This is the place of terror," he said. "And here you will know terror! It is in this room that your fellow heretic confessed all, and it is here that you, too, shall confess all. How many and who! Those you have given your body like a woman, and those with whom you practiced unholy rites against Heaven. Their names and dates and all that shall be needed for the trial. When you have done that and have truly repented of your sinfulness, then you shall be burned alive at the stake; and by the purifying influence of the flames, it may be that your soul shall be saved and allowed to enter into the bliss of a heavenly reward."

I licked my lips, looking around the room.

"And if I confess now?"

"It will do no good, for you might be merely confessing to save yourself from the torture. If that were the case, then you would not be truly repentant and your soul would not be saved. You *must* be put to the torture, for your own good. A man confessing under the torture is seldom insincere!"

I felt anger boil up in me.

"It could not be that you have wages to protect, or are concerned with the steady income the Crown receives from the confiscation of the estates of the heretics, now could it?" I asked. "It could not be that you have run out of true heretics and witches, could it, and depend on the innocent to point the finger at other innocents, so that your coffers can continue to grow?"

"No man or woman," the Inquisitor said gravely, "has ever left these walls without confessing. Who am I to doubt the truth that God puts into my hands? If there are any innocents among those I have burned, then God has shown little inclination to save them, as he did the innocents in the fiery furnace. If I am left the choice of deciding who is innocent and who is guilty, I am more than content to let the choice rest with the Almighty and follow the orders of the Holy Father in Rome. As to innocence, you might remember that it was a Pope named Innocent who began the Inquisition. Therefore do not be deceived that innocence will save you!"

He led me to an alcove of the torture chamber and showed me what was there, more to instill fear in me than to prepare me for it.

"This is the ladder," he said. "Observe how it works. You are strapped to it, your feet over the bottom, your hands over the top. The rungs of the ladder are sharpened, not so sharp as knives, but sharp enough to cut. You are stretched on it, like the rack, and the rungs cut into your back, deeper as you are stretched tighter."

The man who was strapped to the ladder was still conscious, and his eyes bespoke the pain the device provided. I felt more pity for him at that moment than terror for my own estate. The blood trickled down his naked back where the rungs had cut into him.

I was led to another alcove, and here a man was fastened down to a kind of board bed. His neck and wrists were fastened by a kind of stocks to the head of this bed; his feet were fastened through another such stock at the foot.

"This is the bastinado," said the Inquisitor, picking up a long rod of birch, about two inches thick. "It is a simple device, but effective."

With all the force he could muster he rapped the cane across the soles of the man's feet, and the man screamed. With increasing violence he repeated the procedure, beating the bare soles of the man's feet till I was sure the bones must be broken. Then he stopped.

"When a man has had the arches broken and the bones of his feet, he is then ready to walk!" said the Inquisitor. "Sometimes he will merely walk though the streets to the stake. Sometimes he will walk to the next torture!"

He led me to another alcove. Here was another table, and on it another man strapped down. On the outside of each leg a strong wooden plank was fastened to the table. Between his legs were two more such planks, not fastened down. Between the two center boards wedges had been driven, so that the inner planks were slowly and inexorably driven outward, crushing his legs against the outer ones. By this method the knee bones had been crushed.

I did not know whether he was alive or dead at first, for the knees looked swollen like those of an overripe corpse; but as I looked, I observed that he breathed, and uttered a prayer under my breath that he would not do so for long.

As we approached the next alcove, I saw a sight that made me cringe back and turned my stomach at the same time. A man was strapped into a chair, his bare feet placed in large metal boots set on the floor before him. As I watched, a torturer came forward from the forge in the center of the room and poured from a glowing crucible on a rod molten lead into the boots. The man screamed such a scream as I had never heard, and the true terror of the Inquisition came home to me.

In another alcove a man hung by his thumbs over a fire. A man who seemed to enjoy what he was doing held a bunch of feathers coated in sulphur under the man's arm-pits, then under his crotch, and set fire to them.

The sulphur vaporized and its thick yellow smoke went up and clung to the tender flesh, like a liquid fire, as the poor man shrieked. His torturer laughed as he writhed back and forth, pulling his thumbs out of their sockets in his pain.

"This is only the beginning," said the Inquisitor. "This is only the most popular level of our ingenuity. These are things any small-town torturer could do. We have darker means at our disposal as well. Things more terrible than these by far. We have had two hundred years to learn how to make men's souls what we want them to be. In that time we have sent to Heaven so many that you cannot comprehend it. In France alone, four hundred thousand. In Germany, six hundred thousand. In Spain, a tiny two hundred thousand; but the Spanish Inquisition has shown much ingenuity in its methods! Now do you quail before the power of the Lord? Now do you see what power I hold?"

"You are the Devil himself!" I spat at him.

"I am the servant of God," he said. "Before the Inquisition crimes were punishable by death, but the sinner went to Hell. Now we have a chance of sending him to Heaven. Strip him!"

These last words were directed to the guards, who ripped the pants and hose from me and dragged me to the next alcove. I tried to fight back, but with my arms bound I was helpless as they lifted me to a long, flat table and bound my feet with ropes to rings at its bottom.

Thus secured, they untied my arms and bound my wrists with more rope, these ropes ending by being wound around a huge drum some six feet distant from my finger tips as they stretched me out. This was the rack!

The Inquisitor signaled and a young man in a monk's robe came up, a quill and writing box with parchment at the ready in his hand.

"Now we will begin," the Inquisitor said. "Slowly, and carefully, so that we can understand every word you say. The rack will stretch you and stretch you and you will feel your joints slowly part as your muscles are torn apart. You will tell me whom you have committed sins with, particularly the sin of sodomy, and with whom you have celebrated the infamous Black Mass, and such other evil rites as the witches and Jews practice. You will give me details of these acts, so that they may be brought forth in court. You will tell me where the heretics live, that I may have them arrested and brought here. All this you will do at my bidding! And beyond that, you will *repent!*"

He signaled, and the guards began to turn the big drum, wrapping the ropes tighter around it.

My arms first were lifted off the table, and the ropes dragged me upward. Then the ropes around my ankles caught and held me, and I began to stretch. The tension lifted my whole body off the table, and I began to feel the slow tearing in half that is the only subtlety of the rack.

As I lay suspended in the air, stretched between ropes at either end, my body slowly being torn, I felt a hand upon my chest. I lifted my head and saw that the Inquisitor was stroking me; then felt him begin to play with my right nipple.

"You will tell me all these things," he said softly, and the familiarity of the voice was so great that I felt I must burst unless I knew it. He played with my other nipple, then slid his hand down my belly and began to toy with my cock, and then my balls. The rack stretched me tighter, and I felt like screaming; but I also felt my cock starting to get hard.

He slid his hand between my legs and slid a finger up my ass. The rack stretched me tighter.

"Who are you, you devil?" I cried.

He slid his finger out and slowly stroked my body, moving up it all the way as guards turned the drum of the infernal machine, stretching me, pulling me apart. The pain was so great I barely heard him as he whispered his long, aristocratic Spanish name, a name that struck real terror into my heart.

He reached up and pushed the great peaked hood back from his head, and I looked into his dark eyes, eyes filled with betrayal and a lust so unnatural that I could not endure to think how I had fallen into his clutches. I looked upon his face, once so admired and respected that I had loved him for it.

"Ramon, Viscount d'Esposa!" I cried.

"You see," he said. "This is *not* the beginning! Our love was the beginning. But neither is this the end. I have much more I will do with you!"

I shrieked as the rack grew tighter, and I looked into a face that was two faces at once. One, the face of the lover who had betrayed me: the other the face of my sergeant, so far now in the future, and so beloved.

Twelve

I awoke from my dream with the marks of intravenous feeding on my arms, feeling better than I had for a long time. Centuries, I thought at first. The images of the Inquisition were fresh in my mind as I lay in the clean infirmary bed, naked between the clean white sheets. It had been my religious training, of course, that had led me to dream thus; a terrible, true dream, filled with the realities of long ago.

But not so long ago enough, I thought as I lay there. Not so long that the same kind of men were not alive and practicing. And not just the Hitlers or the Napoleons, either. Every man or woman who used some form of coercion to force another to their viewpoint was a potential Inquisitor, different only in degree of coercion available to them.

The corpsmen must have kept me out with drugs until they felt I was ready, then given me a stimulant to bring me around. I had not been awake long when my sergeant and the two corporals came for me, telling me that I was well over my 'inconvenience' and that I was ready to continue my training.

I was clean, so they didn't bother to take me to the showers. They marched me straight to the room with the mirrors, where the usual groups of men were being exercised. I was taken to one corner, stealing a glance as I went, to see if Fido was there (he was), and set to work doing pushups, leg lifts, sit-ups, and other basic calisthenics.

After so long an interval, plus however long I'd lain in bed after passing out in the latrine, it was another kind of agony.

"Navy boys never do get much exercise," the redheaded corporal drawled as I sweated. "Not like the Marine Corps training, not at all. Man, you're a Marine, you *work!* Like they say, the Marine Corps builds men! Looks like the Navy builds nelly faggots!"

He laughed, and so did all the other Marines in the room. The rest of us were too busy trying to do our exercises, after whatever privations we had endured.

I thought the exercises were going to kill me. I didn't have the strength to get through them. But whenever I collapsed they would just let me lie there for a while, then switch me to another set of muscles. There were barely any traces of the welts my body had registered from the beatings, but now all the pain was back, this time inflicted from the inside out.

The enforced exercise went on for a long time. I noticed that some of the groups left and others entered. Once during that first day a man was brought in and set to work on Fido, licking him the way I had licked him. I felt a hard-on start, but it didn't get anywhere because I was too exhausted to keep my attention on what I was doing and on what was happening to Fido.

They eventually returned me to my cell, which was now much cleaner and cooler. When supper came, I was surprised to find a steak, mashed potatoes, green beans and a salad. There was even a glass of milk. I wolfed it down, then regretted it.

My stomach was so unused to solid food like this that I puked it right back up.

I sat on the edge of my bed for a while, thinking that I had been played another trick, the sweat cooling on my forehead after the vomiting. Was I never going to learn that nothing good could happen to me? Just then the trap at the bottom of my cell door clattered and another try with the same items slid in.

I stared at it for a while, then decided, what-the-hell, if I puked it up again, that was that. I would still enjoy eating it, and besides, if I ate more slowly and sensibly I might even retain it.

That meal was the beginning of a new phase in my training. Where before they had sought to break me down, now they began to build me up. They worked on my body as if they were working on a prize athlete. They fed me better than officers usually ate. It puzzled me at first, but then I realized they were all calling me 'Rover' now, and that I was not being trained like a prize athlete, but like a show dog.

My time sense was gone, and it didn't occur to me to try and keep track of sequences any more. I exercised when they told me to, I ate when food was offered. I washed, sometimes being scalded, sometimes not. They took me to a barber and he shaved my face and gave me a neat, military haircut. Now when I walked into the room with mirrors, I wasn't embarrassed by my own reflection. I was beginning to look like myself once more.

One day they took me for a walk outside the building. It was early in the morning, I discovered, just near dawn. It had been so long since I'd seen real sunlight that it hurt my eyes. Even the fresh air felt alien on my skin.

We walked in a walled compound, not unlike any other prison exercise compound, except that along one wall was a series of low cages. In the cages there were naked men, each with a chain dog collar around his neck. The cages weren't high enough for the men to stand upright, so when they moved around they had to do so on their hands and knees. There was a cement floor to each cage, and at one end a trough in which some particularly unappetizing food was slung. There was also a trough with water in it.

"The kennels," said the dark corporal, confirming my guess. "Any dog who's caught trying to eat with his paws is whipped. After a while they learn to eat the way dogs should."

I could see that some of the men must have been in the cages for a long while, because there were piles of excrement on the floors of the cages. I shuddered, thinking of Fido's superb body confined to this kind of punishment. I vowed that I would never do anything to deserve it, no matter how tempting it might be.

The next day I had a chance to test my resolve. As I was brought into the room with mirrors, Fido was being taken out by his keeper, the poor animal in tears. What he had done they didn't tell me. They only told me that I was to take his place.

They took me to where the rod with the vibrating dildo projected up from the floor. I could see it fully now, and it frightened me. It seemed to be even larger than the dark corporal's cock. It looked for all the world like a real penis, except that it was on the end of a pole sticking up from the floor instead of attached to a man.

The sergeant took a can of white grease and gingerly rubbed some up my ass with two of his fingers. He then greased the big dildo thoroughly. That was much more than anyone had done for me while they were raping me, so I was properly grateful to him.

They checked my height and made some adjustment, one that left the thing still too tall for me to consider; and then they were satisfied. I noticed that a ceiling panel had slid back, and that there was a block and tackle up inside it. They lowered a rope, bound my hands with it, and hoisted me up.

The strain of being lifted by my arms made me think of the rack in my dream. There was no more real tension on me than if I'd been hanging from a set of school yard athletic bars, but the fact that I couldn't let go made it seem like there was. They moved me over the dildo and began to slowly lower me, stopping while they positioned the head of the thing at my asshole.

"Hope you can remember to relax," smiled the sergeant, playing with my cock a little. My cock was now hard, as I felt it should be under the circumstances.

They released the rope a little at a time, lowering me onto the big plastic cock. They were not trying to hurt me this time, just preparing me for a show. I was like a dog being groomed. And that helped some. I did try to relax my anal sphincter as best I could. But the thing was just too big, and as I settled down onto it helplessly, I felt as if I was going to be split open.

That led me to squirming, and that in turn let me slip down onto it a little more. I began to moan, the sheer size of it incomprehensible as it slid deeper and deeper up my ass.

"I survived the dark corporal," I thought to myself. "If I could do that, I can do this!"

But now I began to understand what impaling was all about. If it was done with a spear, you died horribly and slowly, unable to escape. Done this way you didn't die, but you were just as helpless to escape. Because you couldn't raise yourself off the thing shoved deep inside you.

Long past the time I felt I couldn't take any more I felt my feet touch the ground, first my toes, then my heels. I felt the rope slacken, and then they took the ropes off my wrists and hid them all away up in the ceiling, the mirror panel sliding back neatly.

I opened my eyes and looked around, and realized that I was now the center of attention. I stood there, the huge dildo up my ass, impaled on it, mirrors on all sides, my own image reflected hundreds of times. And everyone in the room was looking at me. I looked at myself, reflected back from the mirrors, and I was astonished at my own image.

I wasn't the ideal that Fido had been, but I was not bad looking at all. I could imagine some slave coming into the room, seeing himself wrecked as I had been, and slavering over me as an object of lust. The pubic hair was nearly all grown back, even my chest was starting to get bushy again. My muscles were filling back in a little, and if they kept exercising me, I would look pretty good pretty soon.

I wondered how long Fido had been kept on show, impaled in the exercise room. And what kind of indiscretion had taken him out this time.

"Throw the switch," said my sergeant.

The redhead walked over to the wall and flipped what looked like a light switch, but it wasn't. It was the switch controlling the vibrator inside the dildo, inside me. And it was no lightweight vibrator like the one they'd used on me before. It was powerful, like the kind of thing a barber puts on his hand to massage your scalp. I was galvanized by it, paralyzed with the sensations it produced, and I reached automatically for my cock as it sent waves of vibration into it.

The sergeant brushed aside my hand, and I had to force myself to focus on him, so overwhelming was the pleasure I was feeling inside my guts.

"You're not here to enjoy yourself, Rover. You're here to serve others and to learn discipline. You touch your cock or any other cock you're not told to touch, and you go to the kennels outside. Now you just stand there and be a good dog and everything will be fine. Maybe you'll even get a reward!"

My mind spun off in all directions and I did the only thing I could think of, the thing I'd seen Fido do before me. I put my hands behind me and locked them together, as if they were tied. Then I gave myself up to the cloud of desire that the vibrator was producing in my balls and cock, stimulating my prostate through the intestinal wall.

I began to pray, not to God exactly, but more to my sergeant. I prayed that he would let me come. I prayed that he would say the word that would let me shoot my load. I prayed that he would let somebody suck me off, the way I'd sucked Fido.

After a while I felt something by my feet and opened my eyes to see a young man on his knees, beginning to lick between my toes. I had never thought of my toes as erotic, but the touch of his tongue went through me like an electric current and I moaned.

He worked his way up, just as I had done, and I went crazy, writhing on the pole and making it twist inside me; and that shoved the vibrator up against my prostate even more, and I writhed even more. I couldn't conceive that it had been this way for Fido. He had been here a long time. Even an hour was too much for me. Many moments more and I was sure I would lose my mind with pleasure.

He got to my balls and started to lick them. I screamed and thrashed and begged for the sergeant to say the word. I could see his black eyes smiling at me as if through a mist, and I felt shame that I was disgracing him by my behavior even while I realized that I wasn't disgracing him, I was proving excellent in training men to beg.

The boy started to lick my cock.

"I can't, I *can't!*" I whimpered to my sergeant.

"You have to!" he replied.

He got to the head and took it in his mouth, running his tongue around the head.

"Please, Sir! *Please!*"

"No!"

"Then *whip* me, Sir! Something, anything. *Whip me!*"

He yanked the boy's mouth off my cock and pulled him away from me. I twisted, going up on my toes, then dropping myself onto the huge dildo, fucking myself with it.

"Come!" the sergeant said, and I did.

Thirteen

The sergeant was so pleased with me that he gave me a collar of my own. A metal chain collar, a dog collar, soldered around my neck. I even had a little tag that said 'Rover' on it.

They continued to exercise me brutally, making me do more and more pushups, lift more and more weights, and, most important, more leg lifts and more sit-ups. I began to develop that washboard stomach I had never even thought about acquiring.

Sometimes they would hoist me up and impale me, putting me on show, and at the same time in a position of temptation. Just standing there with the big vibrating dildo inside me was rough, but having to control myself while some newcomer was licking and sucking me was agony. Yet the sweetest agony I had ever known! I developed an intense and constant feeling that was like an apotheosis of that pride you get when you have just graduated from boot camp. A feeling that Hell was worth it. And I somehow maintained my self-control, never once doing what the sergeant told me not to do.

The sergeant began to take me around with him, just the way you would let a well-behaved dog go places with you. He taught me to sit quietly: well, not exactly sit, for that didn't suit him. I squatted when he said sit, so that my legs were spread and my cock and balls always hanging down and exposed. That way, he explained, if I got a hard-on, anybody could see it. A dog, after all, is not supposed to have any privacy at all. His every action is subject to whatever notice or commentary the humans around him might wish to make.

At first the sergeant only took me out to the yard and had me sit while he checked on the other dogs. He wasn't the one who fed them or watered them, but he seemed to be somehow in charge of them. He would call them over to the side of the cage and scratch their heads or speak softly to them. I think, now that I look back, that he still treated me more like a human than he did them; but I couldn't tell. My paramount concern was to maintain my status with him, so that I wasn't put in a cage like they were.

I remember how once one of the dogs started yelling at him and calling him names. He quietly walked over and got a garden hose and sprayed the guy, which was a pretty rough thing to do, being as night was coming on and the temperature was going down. He didn't spray him with force, just a spray that would get him good and wet. He also made sure the piles of shit were soaked, so they would smell and attract flies.

He also told the guy that next time he would wash all the shit down into the feeding trough, where it would stay until it was cleaned out. I understood what he meant by that, and renewed my resolve to stay out of the kennels.

Fido was down at one end, and I know I stared at him openly. He avoided looking at me, or maybe he didn't remember me any more than I could remember the men who had sucked me while I was impaled. The sergeant called me over, though, and said: "Here, boy, you remember Fido, don't you?"

"Sir! Yes, Sir!" I replied.

"Well, good! You've been taking his place for a while, and you know, he probably misses it. Why don't you suck him off, eh, Rover? I think he'd like that."

I looked Fido in the eye, wondering what to do. I certainly had no objection to sucking him off, even if he was a little dirty and shabby from being in the kennels. I felt a deep kinship with him. After all, we'd both had the same big thing up our asses, as well as having had a sort of sex together.

He had a haunted look in his eyes, and I wondered what things had been done to him, possibly worse than what had been done to me. Suddenly, I felt a deep and overwhelming compassion for Fido, and I wanted, more than anything, to help him in his misery. I could tolerate what was happening to me, because a man learns to endure hardship. But to see it happening to somebody else, that is in a lot of ways much harder.

"Would you like me to suck you?" I asked Fido.

"What was that?" asked the sergeant, danger in his voice.

I became confused.

"I said . . ." I began, but he cut me off.

"I thought you'd learned, when we were whipping you, that there isn't any 'I' in your vocabulary!"

I crumbled. I didn't even know how to apologize. I wished that I truly had a tail to hang between my legs, so that I could show him how sorry I felt without saying anything.

"You'll be punished for that!" he said.

"Yes, Sir!" I responded, almost too quiet to be heard.

"Come here!" he said.

I followed him out into the center of the yard, and he told me to lie face down on the grass. I lay there for what seemed like a very long time, then he was beside me. He drove a spike into the ground, through my collar, so that I was pinned down by the neck. Then he went away again.

A few minutes later I heard him come back.

"All right, Blue," he said. "You've been a good dog. There's your reward, now take him!"

I didn't even have time to be afraid. There was a big man, muscular and broad shouldered, on top of me, and I felt his cock pushing into my ass. There was no grease, not even spit, and he wasn't gentle. He just shoved in, dry and hard, and I moaned.

It was a good thing that I'd had all that training with the dildo. My ass had loosened up a lot, and I had learned how to relax. The surprise of it made it hurt at first, but once he'd rammed it in, I was all right.

He fucked me hard and crazily, as if he'd been waiting for weeks. He panted and sweated furiously as he fucked, faster than I'd ever been fucked. When he came it was a savage release, with no trace of anything but relief in it. I realized that there had been a great deal of personality in the fucking I'd got from the Marines. Each one of them had been personally involved in what he was doing. Blue was just an animal in rut!

The sergeant took Blue back to his cage, and I lay there on the grass with the sun beating down on me. It didn't seem as if the punishment had been too bad. I didn't want to admit to myself, even then, that I had actually sort of enjoyed it. But then, the sergeant hadn't meant it to be a complete punishment. In a moment he was back with another dog, this one with a much bigger bone to bury in my asshole.

It occurred to me that the sergeant was going to have all the dogs who'd been waiting for a reward to fuck me.

I didn't know how many of them there were, but I figured there must have been at least ten. And as Number Two, who name was King, shoved his big boner in, I knew that it was not going to be fun, by any means!

He fucked me the same way Blue had; impersonally, hard and fast. I felt as if my ass was just a socket into which things got plugged. But a socket doesn't get worn out, and I wondered how much I could take before I did get worn out.

I was sweating by the time King finished, and then came Spot, who got a twist of the knife every time they called him because he was black. He had a tool even bigger than King's, and he used it more voraciously. I figured, as he shot his stinging load into me, that I was getting the anger of a hundred years of bigotry more than anything that might be thought of as 'love'!

I lost track of the names of the animals who fucked me, and there was never any consideration of their personalities; the whole point of the 'dog' exercise was to remove any trace of personality. The only thing I can remember from the last part of it was a whisper at my ear. I had never heard Fido's voice, but I knew it was him, ramming his cock into me like all the rest, and probably praying that the sergeant wouldn't notice him speaking as he bit my ear to cover his speaking. He said as he bit and bucked me: "I'm sorry!"

My ass was sore as hell, and I'm sure the sergeant took special delight the next day in having me impaled. I figured he had been waiting for me to make a mistake for some time, and I realized that however much pride he might take in my successful training, he took pleasure in having a chance to reprimand me.

One morning my breakfast didn't arrive, then no lunch. I was really hungry by the time they came to put me through my exercises. After the exercises I was starving, and would happily have gone for whatever was in one of those food troughs in the kennels. I was impaled for a while, and the pleasure of being vibrated while I was sucked off a couple of times took some of the edge off the hunger. But when they slid me off the dildo, everything started to look edible.

They marched me down the endless halls again, and this time they took me into another section I'd never visited. This section had varnished wooden doors with little brass plates with numbers on them. It was an old part of the building; but it was very well-kept, and it didn't take me long to figure out that I was in officers' territory.

I wondered if I should salute, but the first time my hand came up, the sergeant knocked it down again. I realized that there could be nothing sillier than a naked man wearing a metal dog collar saluting. For that matter, the idea of a dog saluting was even sillier!

The two corporals left us at a set of double doors, and the sergeant explained to me.

"This is the officers' mess," he said. "You're going to be the table dog today. Your job is to keep out of sight, and keep your sights on the floor. If anything falls, you scramble over and eat it, real quick. You understand?"

"Sir! Yes, Sir!" I said, feeling only that I was going to get something to eat, at last.

"And you don't use your paws!"

"Sir! Yes, Sir!" I repeated.

He took me through the door, and I was in the officers' mess.

"Sit!" the sergeant commanded, and I squatted beside him, just inside the door. "And stay on your hands and knees," he added in a whisper.

The officers were all Marines as I should have guessed they would be. They took no notice of either the sergeant or me, and I should have realized that, too. They ate and talked, and looking back, I might have gained a lot of insight into the workings of the Brig if I had just listened. But I was so hungry by that point that my only interest was looking between their feet at the floor around the several tables.

I wondered if they would ever drop anything. After all, one doesn't expect officers of any service to be slovenly. The idea that I could make a meal on what fell from their plates was unlikely. But then, I reminded myself, this was not an ordinary group of officers. They would be doing things that were outside the ordinary. They would be doing things that were part of the training. And also things to test me, to see if they could make me acquire demerits and punishments.

A piece of chicken fell to the floor and I scrambled over on my hands and knees to get it. I almost grabbed it with my fingers, then remembered. It flashed across my mind that chicken was probably a test. Nobody eats chicken with anything but fingers, except maybe rich people in restaurants, where it comes all covered with sauce. I hunkered down and got it with my teeth and started to eat it.

Something hit me that I hadn't expected to matter. I realized that I was eating something that had just been in a stranger's mouth.

I started to gag, one of those old responses that your parents build into you when they are trying to save you from germs. Then I mastered it, almost laughing when I thought of all the piss I'd drunk and all the cocks I'd sucked. Still, it felt strange to be eating food that had just been in a stranger's mouth; especially one whose face I'd never even seen. For indeed, my eyes remained on the floor, where the food would fall, just as a good dog's eyes should!

I ate as much of the chicken off the bone as I could, then wondered what I should do with the bone. If I dropped it where I was, I might be scolded or punished. If I asked where to put it But that was ridiculous: dogs don't ask, they just . . .

I went back over by the door and squatted down, and started to chew on the bone.

Another something hit the floor, at the other end of the room, and I dropped the bone from my mouth. I hurried to where I'd heard the sound and began lapping up some creamed spinach. It was more than a mouthful, so I knew it was deliberately dropped. There's no way you can lift a gob of creamed spinach that big into your mouth. It got all over my cheeks, and I tried to lick it off; but then I heard some more food, and went after that.

I realized, after a while, that they were laughing at me. But it didn't seem to matter. I was so much in the state of mind that the sergeant had cultivated, so driven by conditioning and hunger, that I would have been happy to do any tricks they wanted, so long as I kept eating. The morsels I was getting were small ones, and it looked like a long time before I could make up the difference between my steak and potatoes regular meals and what I was licking up off the floor in the officers' mess.

I finished eating a piece of buttered bread, and started as I felt someone scratch my back. I looked up, and in the chair above me I saw a colonel, his face tough but handsome, grey at his temples, a salt and pepper mustache topping a hard mouth.

"Nice dog you've got, Sergeant," he said, reaching up and scratching behind my ears.

"Thank you, Sir!" the sergeant replied, back by the door.

I found that I liked the way he scratched my head. I wished that I had a tail, so that I could wag it. Then I knew what to do, and licked his hand.

The other Marines at the table laughed, and so did the colonel, but he also smiled down at me.

"Does it do any tricks?" the colonel asked.

"Yes, Sir!" said the sergeant.

"Good!" said the colonel. "Send it around to my quarters after dinner."

He patted me on the head, then reached down and gave me a little piece of half-chewed meat. I took it in my mouth and wolfed it down and licked his hand again. But then he seemed to forget that I was there, and went back to his conversation.

I got to lick the whipped cream from several of the dessert dishes that night, and was very pleased with myself when the sergeant showered me, scalding, and took me to the colonel's quarters. The sergeant, too, seemed pleased.

The colonel had me suck him off several times in a row, then fucked me twice. I was amazed at the prowess the man had, so late in life; but then, I was very young and inexperienced and didn't know much about 'older men.' Looking back, I think the colonel was probably in his early or middle forties, and that isn't late for a dominant type of man.

But, being an officer, he didn't allow me to sleep on the bed.

Fourteen

I adjusted pretty well to my life as a dog. I suppose that whatever had happened to me while I was sick from the routine in the latrine might have helped. But there was also the fact that I wasn't getting whipped every day. The absence of pain can be just as powerful a stimulus as the presence of pain.

I exercised. I was impaled, and that kept my ass in shape for getting fucked. I was sucked, and I did a lot of sucking. Sometimes I made mistakes, and there were punishments; but none of them was as bad as the whipping in the room with the wooden table. Sometimes I was table dog, but after that first time, they didn't starve me so badly; they just let me miss one meal beforehand, so that I'd be sure and do a good job cleaning up.

Various officers had me to their rooms at night, and I learned a number of sexual practices that were not exactly torture, but were definitely not usual. I found that I was very much pleased to please them.

It seemed to me that I must be doing well with my training. I no longer required three Marines for a guard all the time. Sometimes only two of them would come for me in the morning, and then, only one. I suppose that allowed the others to be reassigned to some more important duty.

One morning it was the dark corporal who came to fetch me. I still feared him more than the other two, and still responded, I thought, more quickly to his commands than to any other. I genuinely loved the sergeant, now, but I still feared the dark corporal for the power he was willing to put into his punishments.

He took me down for a scalding shower, then, instead of taking me to the room with mirrors, he brought me back to my cell. To my surprise, my Navy uniform was lying on the bed.

"Put it on!" he ordered, matter-of-factly. "I'm taking you down for release."

I didn't know how to react. I think I'd forgotten what release meant. Did he mean that my discharge had come through? Did he mean that they were going to let me out of the Brig? Had my eight weeks finished?

I put on the uniform, shabbily I am sure. It had been a long time since I'd worn any clothes at all. I didn't have a mirror, and my fingers trembled as I tried to tie the tie.

He walked me along the corridors and my mind swam. I thought about the world outside. What was it really like? Were my memories any good? How would I be able to relate to it? I wasn't a man any more, only a dog. I had come in a nice straight boy: now I was as queer as a three-dollar bill, a slave, an animal.

I thought about the girl I was almost engaged to. And it hit me, like cold water after the scalding shower, that I hadn't thought about her since I'd come into the Brig. I wondered if it had been self-defense, or if it had been because, deep down inside, I had always been queer. After all, she and I had never made it. She was a nice Puerto Rican girl, Catholic, and they didn't do it before marriage.

I almost laughed as I found myself using all the old clichés. I could think quite clearly about being sucked and fucked, and a lot of other things...with men. But thinking about just plain fucking, with my almost-fiancée, was beyond me still!

I think I must have been crying a little when I realized that the dark corporal had brought me to the lounge. It was like coming to after being out cold. There I was, standing and looking at myself in the mirror on the cloakroom door. A not-unhandsome sailor, not very neatly dressed, and looking a little dazed.

"Strip!" the dark corporal said.

I looked at him, in the mirror, and then full comprehension came.

"You're not releasing me!" I cried out, the tears breaking from my eyelids.

For the first time, the dark corporal really smiled. His broad, sensuous mouth stretched wide over beautiful white teeth. His hazel eyes gleamed. His handsome, lean features took on a glow that made his olive skin shine like bronze at sunrise.

"No," he said, and for once it seemed that what he was doing was not just a job, but something he was really enjoying.

I stripped, still staring at him in the glass, still shaken at my own stupidity in believing I was going to escape. When my chest was bare I realized how really stupid I had been. If they were going to release me, they would certainly have taken the dog collar off!

"I want you to play in the mirror," he said when I was naked. "I want you to look at yourself, and see yourself for what you really are, at every moment of this little exercise. You understand?"

"Sir! Yes, Sir!" I replied.

"Good. Now put this on!"

He tossed me a garment covered with bright pink and purple orchids, a garment slippery and cool to the touch. I unfolded it and saw it was a dress. Was this what I had come to? I slipped it over my head, let it fall down over my shoulders, and adjusted it around my hips, trying to make it look right as I gazed at myself in the mirror. If anything in the imprisonment had been humiliating, this was worse. Before, they had taken away my manhood and made me a slave, then an animal. Now they wanted me to become a woman!

"Prance around in it!" the corporal smirked. "Show me how a faggot behaves!"

I tried to do what he asked. I knew that if I failed him there would be some awful punishment, but I didn't really care. At least being whipped was something a man could deal with. I didn't want to lose the last scrap of manhood I had; but that was what was happening, right before me in the mirror.

"Now, lisp a little, faggot!" he laughed.

"Thir! Yeth, Thir!" I lisped.

He roared with laughter.

"Now, tell me, right there in the mirror: what's a Navy faggot good for? And lisp it!"

"Thucking cock, Thir, and getting fucked!"

And that sounded so silly that I started laughing, too. It was laughter out of humiliation, rather than humor, and I knew the corporal was laughing at me, not with me; but it was still ridiculous. I looked at myself, absurd in the filmy dress; with its padded shoulders, its big, blotchy orchids, it was clearly something left over from the forties. I wondered if it was something his mother had worn.

"Wiggle your hips a little," he said.

I did it.

"Pretend you're a cootch dancer!"

I tried that, too.

"Pull it down over your shoulder, the way Marilyn Monroe used to do!"

I did it, and even winked at him in the mirror.

"Want to suck my cock?" he asked.

"Thir! Yeth, Thir!" I responded, foolishly.

He stood up and opened his pants. His enormous cock and huge balls flopped out.

"Come on!" he said, walking over to me. I knelt down in front of him and took the end of it in my mouth.

"Keep looking in the mirror," he said. "I want you to know what you look like sucking cock!"

I was almost sideways to the mirror, but not quite. His back was slightly to it, so it was no real problem for me to look at what I was doing.

It was fascinating to see it.

There I was, wearing the dress, on my knees, and there was his firm ass, hairy and tight, reflected in the glass. The sides of his legs were reflected, too, and his big balls, slapping against my chin. I had almost forgotten how hard it was to stretch my mouth that wide and take it in; how hard it was to loosen my throat enough for it to go down.

I sucked, and the spittle started drooling down my chin. I guess that happened often, but I had never seen it happen before. I had never seen my own face with a cock fucking it. I got really hard, watching it happen. And I could see my hard-on sticking straight out, making a tent on the front of my filmy skirt. The silky material felt good, rubbing across the head of my cock.

As he fucked my mouth, the corporal stripped to the waist, exposing his smooth, golden chest, the long black hairs that grew around his big, brown nipples, the perfect symmetry of his washboard stomach. I remembered how much I had admired that stomach the first time I had seen it. How much I had wanted one like it. And how much I had been afraid to admit that to myself. Maybe, I thought, if they keep training me, I will get one that good, eventually.

The smell of his crotch was wonderful, and I began to get the smell of his sweaty armpits, too. He hadn't sweated much, before. It occurred to me that he was really enjoying what I was doing for him, and I sucked even harder.

He took my head in his hands and slowly, carefully, drew it off his cock.

"Stand up!" he commanded, smiling.

I stood up.

"Now bend over and grab your ankles," he said. "But keep on watching in the mirror!"

I did what he said, and he lifted up my skirt, exposing my ass to view. He took his big, wet, slippery cock and started to slide it up my ass. It was still the biggest cock I'd ever taken, but it was not so big as the dildo they kept me impaled on. I took it, if not easily, at least with pleasure. I knew how much I enjoyed it, not only by what it felt like, but by my own face reflecting ecstasy in the mirror.

I watched fascinated as the huge tool slid in and out of me. It was like watching some giant piston on a powerful machine. Some huge, well-oiled rod, plunging deep in and returning as the flywheel turned. I felt the passion building in me, my own balls swinging back and forth inside the skirt, my own hard cock banging against my belly as he fucked me harder and harder.

"Tell me how much you like getting fucked, faggot," he said as he fucked me.

"I love it!" I said, forgetting that I wasn't supposed to use the personal pronoun. "I love getting fucked! I love having your big dick up my ass, Sir! It's the best dick I ever had; the biggest and the best, Sir! I love the way you use it, Sir, and I want it! Oh, fuck me, Sir! Fuck me as much as you want! I want you to fuck me forever, Sir!"

I kept telling him, and he kept fucking me, and the vision of it all happening in the mirror made it all the better. It wasn't silly any more, seeing myself in a dress. It was just one more symbol of how much owned I was, of how much an object I was. And as his tool shoved back and forth inside me, pressing against the intestinal wall, massaging my prostate, bringing me closer and closer to an orgasm I knew I couldn't have without his permission, I knew that this was really what I wanted more than anything else. I knew that I would have been lost if they had really released me. I had been weeping, not because I was once again imprisoned, but because I was once again in a position to be used!

He started ramming it in harder and harder, and I lost the ability to speak. My words trailed off, became garbled, and finally were only moans and groans of pleasure. I held on to my ankles as hard as I could, feeling my cock bounce, feeling my balls bounce, and feeling his tool get bigger and harder as he approached orgasm.

And then he shot!

It was like a cannon going off up my ass, and I writhed with the sheer pleasure of it. I wanted it more than I wanted my own orgasm. I wanted it, and I watched in the mirror as I got it. I watched his body stiffen, the sweat pour off his powerful chest, his hairy ass muscles tighten, the rod ram into my ass. I watched his face contort in the pleasure of violence, like a wrestler straining with a powerful grip. His hazel eyes closed and his eyelids wrinkled up. His mouth opened wide in a grimace of pleasure that was like a grimace of pain. And I heard a roar come out of his throat as he exploded inside me.

He kept his cock inside me when he was finished, still hard. He told me to stand up, and I did, the big, hard tool still in me. He wrapped his powerful, sweaty arms around me and lifted me to one of the big leather chairs, where he slowly turned me over, his cock twisting inside me like a corkscrew.

He turned me upside down, so that I was head down in the chair, his cock still in me, him standing over me. He reached down, so that my chest, my belly, and my groin were laid bare. My legs were straight up now, and if I'd dared lower them, they would have draped over his shoulders at the knees.

He gestured with his head to the mirror. I could just see it from my position, and I watched, fascinated, as he took my hard cock in his hand and slowly started to jack me off.

It was a pleasure such as I have never known. His big dick hadn't softened at all, and occasionally he moved it in me, thrusting it against my prostate. He moved his hand deftly, jacking me faster and faster, and soon I was ready. I started to groan as I felt my orgasm coming, the semen boiling up out of my balls through the channel into my cock.

"Take it in your mouth!' he commanded.

I looked straight up at my cock and opened my mouth. He aimed me straight down and the white drops came shooting out, straight down at my face. Some actually got in my mouth, but a lot spattered on my face. One got in my eye, and burned like hell, but I didn't care. I screamed with the pleasure of it.

When he was finished with me he pulled out and let me lie in the chair for a minute or two. Then he went over and opened the door to the cloakroom, the door with the mirror I had been looking into. Behind it were two men wearing marine fatigues. They had a movie camera of some kind.

"The mirror is transparent," said the dark corporal. "Everything is on film. If you ever give us any trouble, the film goes to your parents. They ought to love the part where you're begging me to fuck you forever."

His smile broadened.

Fifteen

I didn't want to be released. Not after that session with the dark corporal and the movie cameras.

While I was in the Brig I was safe from that ultimate humiliation. The one where the world suddenly knew who and *what* I was. In the Brig I would be used; I would be no more than an object of gratification. But in the outside world I would be either in constant danger of exposure, or exposed. Threatened always by the terrible censorship that society focuses on faggots. I would be at the bottom of the heap. Somewhere way down below the ghetto blacks, the chicanos, and the hookers.

Yes, even a whore got a better deal than a queer!

I felt bitter to actually *want* to stay locked up and reduced to the status I had sunk to. But there was still something human in me, and that humanity didn't retreat; it explored. I began to see that anything a human can do is in some sense worth doing, and worth doing well. Before being incarcerated I would have looked with loathing on lots of perfectly ordinary jobs. Not because there was anything awful about them, but because they were the jobs society held in contempt. Now I discovered that even contemptible occupations could be exercised either poorly or well; and that the difference mattered more to the person doing the thing than to Almighty Society.

It struck me with physical force that whether I was queer from the beginning or had been turned queer by the government through the agency of the Marines, it was not my fault! I was who I was, at this moment, and that was what mattered to me. Society, that bitch who so abused me, be damned! I could find satisfaction in whatever task presented itself: that was the essence of my humanity, and that basically was what they wanted to take away. And what I would not give up!

I know this all sounds pretty high-falutin' and intellectual, but I think that is how the mind works. Take it down to the lowest level and it will think; not about what has been poured into it, and not with the patterns it has had impressed upon it, but with a kind of purity, a thinking that looks at things honestly because there is no other way left to look at them.

I decided that it was better to be a good dog, or an excellent cock-sucker, than it was to be a poor-quality politician. It occurred to me that an honest whore does more to benefit society at large than any number of mediocre presidents or senators. Presidents get countries into wars and depressions. The most you can blame on a whore is a few cases of VD.

Given what the government did with biochemistry in Viet Nam, you could even make out a good case for the President being responsible for a hell of a lot of gonorrhea, especially the hard-to-cure epidemic kind!

But gonorrhea was something I didn't have to worry about. The guards at the Brig had all the sex they could handle, and they were the only ones free to bring it in. The medical staff kept close watch on that sort of thing, it being one of the few things the military is good at.

I applied myself to becoming a really good dog. I wouldn't say it was a route to sanity, but it was something that, oddly enough, kept me in touch with being human. I set my mind to really wanting all the things that were expected of me, and I didn't really want to get out. Not any more. After all, it would only mean a life of fear, worrying about whether my parents were going to find out. What would be the point of getting out?

At least in the Brig I was getting lots of sex.

And I realized that I wanted lots of sex. That it had been that basic desire that had alienated me from the ways of the seminary. That the kind of sex I was getting was probably not what I had wanted back then didn't bother me at all. I was an outcast now. I might as well enjoy it!

I did my pushups, my sit-ups, lifted my weights, and stood impaled while some new prisoner worked me over with his mouth. I got sucked, and I got fucked. I did a lot of sucking, too. I let all the problems and realities of the outside world drift away. It became really important to me to do a good job at licking up the spills in the officers' mess. I set out to be the best damned dog they'd ever had.

It occurred to me that men frequently loved their dogs much more than their wives or mistresses, and certainly more than they loved their presidents.

One day the dark corporal came for me alone, and after the scalding shower conducted me to the lounge. I wondered if this was going to be another movie-making session, but of course I couldn't ask. He, however, told me right out.

"You won't know whether they're filming this time or not," he said. "But they may be, so be sure everything you do is visible in the mirror. If they are filming, and you blow it, you'll spend a couple of weeks in the kennels. You understand?"

"Sir! Yes, Sir!"

"Good. Now today is going to be a test. Kind of an obedience test, but a learning test at the same time. You understand?"

"Sir! Yes, Sir!"

"Good. Tell me how much you can remember of what we've done to you."

I was dismayed for a moment, but I wasn't about to fail. I knew that even this was part of a test. It would be hard to answer him without the personal pronoun, but I could try.

"Whipping, Sir!" I said. "And drinking piss, Sir! And sucking cock, Sir! And getting fucked, Sir!"

"Do you think you could put another man through a session like we put you through? But without fucking him, or making him suck you?"

"Sir! Yes, Sir!"

"Think you could do it without any sex at all?"

What was he getting at? Just plain torture?

"Sir! Yes, Sir!"

"Good. That's just what you're going to do! In a minute they're going to bring another guy in. You're going to be the topman in this case, Rover, and you're going to go over him with everything you've got. You're going to take out on him all the resentment you've stored up against us."

He walked across the room and opened a box, and beckoned me to come over beside him.

"In here there are all kinds of toys," he said. "Dildos, tit-clamps, weights, ball-stretchers, whips, belts; you name it. It's all at your disposal. The game is to make this guy come off; but without any actual sexual stimulation. You're going to have to make him come with pain. You understand?"

"Sir! Yes, Sir!" I said, staring at the assortment in consternation. I wondered what the penalty would be if I failed.

"And," said the dark corporal, "you're going to have to do it on your own. There will be only the two of you in here with no one to advise you. You'll have to reach right down in your own mind and dredge up all the stuff you do. You can't blame what happens on anyone else from here on, Rover. The muck is all going to be yours."

That was what I was afraid of. Up to that moment I'd been able to blame someone else for what I was feeling. Now they were putting me on the spot, not only for them, but with myself. Now I would know once and for all what was inside me. And there was no way to escape it, either. It was obvious that if I failed they would find some other way to make me see that dark part of myself. But suppose there was no real, genuine dark part of me to draw from?

"Up here is the hoist," he continued, showing me the ropes that were used to lift a man up off the floor. "There are some nice hot lights here that can really roast a guy, if you think you might like that. The box of candles and the matches I leave to your imagination. And now, Rover, you're on your own."

He slapped my ass hard and, laughing, went out the door. I was alone in the lounge, and I licked the sweat from my upper lip. Was it really that hot, or was I sweating from fear? Was it possible that I was more afraid, standing there alone, than I had been in the presence of the dark corporal?

The door opened again, and someone naked was shoved in. Not ceremoniously accompanied, as I always was, by guards, but just shoved, so that he fell across one of the brown leather chairs. I felt my heart pound. This was to be my victim. I heard the lock on the outside of the door click.

It occurred to me, wildly, that there were just the two of us, both naked; both, I observed, wearing dog collars. What was to stop him from overpowering me? If he could. What if that was the plan? To have us fight it out for control?

Then I recognized him.

It was the black-haired sailor I had seen tortured in the Marine Corps training film!

He looked up and our eyes met. His eyes were beautiful and brown, warm and languid. Under his even black brows they looked like doe's eyes, so helpless, so needful. My heart felt something other than fear. He licked his lips with a pink tongue, the pink contrasting with the bushy black mustache on his upper lip. He was afraid!

I took a deep breath. I didn't know what to say or do. I felt, because I'd seen him in the film, as if he were someone I knew, someone with whom I'd suffered. To make me his torturer was unfair!

"Sir?" he asked, inquisitively.

I wondered how long he had been in the Brig. What he had gone through. A million questions filled my mind. But I also allowed the possibility that he was not what he seemed. That his fear was a ruse, designed to make me fail my test. His fine, masculine beauty was a trap in itself.

I nodded for him to speak, not trusting my voice.

"Sir, it won't matter."

His statement left me blank. What did he mean? I raised one eyebrow, indicating that he should explain.

"Even if you do what they want, Sir," he said, and a look of despair came over him, "even if you do everything to me that they want you to, it won't matter. They'll just keep on torturing you the way they have me. This is just part of the process, Sir. They want you to lose all the self-esteem you have. I know, because I've been here. And I know that I deserve whatever you do to me, because I did it to the man before me. But . . . But you can avoid it, if you just hold out. Oh, they'll torture you some more but they'll do that anyway. You ought to know that by now."

His voice was rising to the point of hysteria. I wondered if he was going to freak out on me, right then and there, and if so, what I could do.

"Don't you see?" he asked passionately, coming to his feet. "It's all lies! They're never going to let any of us out! They're going to drive us crazy with the torture and the pain, and then maybe they'll drive us to suicide, or put us away in mental institutions. Maybe they'll tell our relatives it's shell shock,

I don't know. Please, *please,* please . . ."

I didn't even know what he expected of me. Not to torture him? To help him escape somehow? I wanted to go to him and put my arms around him.

"What do you expect me to do?" I asked at last. My mouth was dry, and it came out harshly, though I didn't mean it that way.

He slumped, standing there. His beautiful brown eyes pleaded with me.

"I don't know," he said dully. "Please don't hurt me any more."

He started to cry.

God! I wanted so much to wrap my arms around him and hold him close to me. I felt all my emotions turning upside down, going crazy. I thought I had found a way of holding on to my sanity. Now all that was lost. I was supposed to torture this man, and I was falling in love with him. Oh, it was crazy; love isn't supposed to be that instantaneous. But under the circumstances, I knew that it was real. Worse, that somehow I had been manipulated. That I was falling in love because the sergeant and the redhead and the dark corporal and Uncle Sam all wanted me to fall in love, and fail my test!

But, I had to ask myself, did that make love any less real?

What was real?

And asking that, I had the answer. The love was real, but it also had no bearing on the situation. Nothing I could do, or not do, was going to change things. If I refused to torture the black-haired sailor, then somebody else would torture him. I could not effect his release. I could only try and find a way to communicate the love I felt while carrying out my orders.

What a monstrous thing to do to a man's mind!

"Look into my eyes," I said softly, but with a firmness that I hoped would satisfy my captors.

The sailor looked, the tears pouring from the brown pools of his eyes and trickling down his cheeks.

"I cannot help you," I said. "Not the way that you have asked me to help you. But I think there is a way that I can . . ." I fumbled for words. "Can make it easier! I am going to torture you; there is no way around that, not for me or you. But . . ."

I swallowed. What I was going to say could make things ten times worse than I'd ever feared. But there was a point where a man was a man, and that was that!

"I'm going to do it with love."

He stared, uncomprehending.

"I want you to try and think about that, while I'm hurting you," I said. "I think it will work. If they can make us respond to pain sexually, then it *will* work. Because sex is a way of expressing love. They always tell us that. Well, if sex is a way of expressing love, then pain can also be a way of expressing it. It won't make it hurt any less, but maybe . . . Maybe you'll be able to feel with each hurt, how much I love you."

His eyes showed me that such sophistry was beyond him, that there was no way he could understand. He had been too much abused to think of pain as anything but pain. And he probably wasn't bright enough to think like a Jesuit on his own.

It hit me at that moment that this whole argument was something I'd picked up in seminary from a Jesuit who'd come to lecture. That too was where the dream of the Inquisition had come from. And now I was doing to this poor sailor what the inquisitors had done to me. Trying to save his soul by harming his body.

I realized that I was fighting not only for my own physical welfare, but suddenly for my soul. Just because they had got to my mind, my sexuality, my sense of reality, they had still not destroyed what I felt was good in me. And now they were trying to get at that!

The test was much more severe than I had thought. I would have to do what was assigned to me, but I would have to do it in such a way that they could find no fault with me and in such a way that I did not destroy myself.

I thought about the cameras that might be grinding away behind the one-way transparency of the mirror. If this was going to be a performance, then I was aiming for an Oscar.

"Come here!" I commanded. I still didn't know whether this was all a trap. Whether at any moment he would turn the tables and laugh at my stupidity.

He walked slowly across the floor. His body was much more beautiful than I had remembered it from the film. I wondered whether it was the exercises they put us through, or whether I was just more susceptible now to masculine beauty.

His curly black hair seemed a little bit longer. His brown eyes glowed with a light that film could never capture. His small nose showed freckles; I wondered if he'd got them in the sunlight, perhaps out in the kennels. There was a day's growth of beard starting to show, a dark shadow to match his mustache, along his firm jaw. His sensual, full lips trembled slightly, probably from the fear that filled his eyes with tears.

As he came close I could smell that fear, an acridness in his sweat. But I could also smell the thick, curly black hair on his broad chest. I couldn't resist reaching out and running my hand over his chest, down the middle, playing with that thick line of hair that spread again into the pubic bush. I wished that I could grab him and hold him against me.

I barely noticed that my cock was hard as a rock. What I felt for the sailor was more than sexual desire, but there was that, too. And as I touched him, he responded, at least as far as the sexual part went. His uncircumcised cock began to grow, swelling slowly, the pink head slowly appearing out of the foreskin like a mushroom pushing up out of the earth. It grew and grew, standing upright, and finally at full attention, in full bloom. I wanted to fall on my knees and devour it.

But the corporal had said to leave the sex out of it. I understood now. All too well, I understood his orders.

If I stood touching him another moment, I would seize him, and that would be that. I felt instinctively that even if they weren't filming, they were watching. If I didn't do what I was supposed to, I knew they would rush in and tear us apart, and then . . .

There was no sense in thinking about it.

I pulled my hand away, looking into his eyes one deep time, hoping that he would somehow understand. Then I went to the chest in the corner.

I found the pair of leather manacles with the sheepskin lining. I remembered seeing them in the film, and I knew they would be there. I brought them back and fastened them on his wrists. I met his eyes once, but the look of loneliness and longing, of pleading and pain, was too much for me to bear. I tore my eyes away and fastened the little buckles securely.

I lowered the ropes from the ceiling and fastened the manacles to them. As long as I did what they wanted me to do, they wouldn't come rushing in. As long as it was me torturing the boy, it wouldn't be someone else.

I realized then that there was a part of me, something very close to the part that desired him, that wanted to torture him. No, not that wanted to torture him. There wasn't any part of me that could identify with my captors, whatever the dark corporal had ordered. Rather, a part that wanted to possess him. To be in control of him, to dominate him, the very same part of a person that seeks to reach out and comfort can seek to reach out and enwrap, take over, enfold. I felt that. I felt the part of me that wanted to fuck him was being rechanneled, like a flood that is forced into a concrete sluiceway. I wouldn't go mad with my desire. I would find another way for it to gain release!

I hauled at the rope and he was lifted up, his strong arms stretched up over his head, the muscles of his chest taut beneath the mat of curly black hair. His muscular legs dangled, and his hard cock stood out. God! How I wanted to walk up to him and suck his cock, now at face level!

I went to the chest and checked through its contents. I could do what my predecessors had done, repeating the performances I'd seen in the film. But I didn't have any boots. That wouldn't work. And I didn't want to do someone else's scene. I wanted to give him what I could of myself in the only way open to me.

I found a little device wrapped in paper and made of leather. There were instructions printed on the paper, explaining how to use it. It was called 'The Seven Gates of Hell.' Somehow it suited my theological frame of mind. I picked it up and went back over to him.

One end of the device was a kind of double ring. It fastened very tightly around the base of his balls. A loop from this part came around and separated his balls up the middle. They stretched very nicely as I fastened it on him, two shiny, hairy globes attached to the body by the compressed flesh within the leather rings. Another loop then went around the base of the cock and balls together, and fastened tightly with a little buckle.

From this second loop a length of leather stretched down the top of the shaft of his cock. There were seven little belts evenly spaced along the length of this piece, each with its own buckle. The one closest to the body I fastened first, tight enough to keep the blood in his cock from flowing back into his body too readily. The second one I fastened a little tighter. Then the third tighter still. By the time I got to the seventh one, which I fastened just under the rim of the head of his cock, the little belt was drawn so tight that it was less than half the diameter of the first one. Now the head of his cock was bright purple with the blood forced into it by the ever-tightening belts and the ever-contracting diameter of his cock as they were tightened. The little paper wrapping assured me that orgasm while wearing this device could be quite painful.

I looked up at his handsome face. His brown eyes stared down at me in fear and still in pleading. But there was already a slight glaze to them, and I knew that he was already sliding over that threshold where pain became pleasure. I found his look exciting and hurried back to the chest.

There were several pairs of tit clamps, some with teeth, some with rubber pads, some with smooth metal clamps. I chose a pair with smooth metal, figuring they would be acceptable to my overseers and would at the same time avoid breaking his skin. I took them back, reached up, and fastened them on his nipples. His head rolled, and he went completely past the threshold. I knew now that he was hurting, but was also beginning to enjoy. I no longer needed to fear what I was doing to him. He would now experience it as a kind of pleasure.

I found myself looking through the chest more carefully now. It was no longer just a show, but something real inside me. I was enjoying what I was doing. I wanted to do it. I wanted to stimulate my captive — my captive! — the way one always wants to stimulate a person one is making love to. And there was no doubt in my mind now: I was making love to the black-haired sailor!

I found some weights with toggle clips and fastened them to the tit clamps, one at a time, watching the clamps pull at his nipples, stretching them down, making them longer and longer, watching them turn white as they were pulled. He writhed back and forth and moaned as I put on each new clip.

The corporal had suggested the lights. I looked them over and found that they were just common sunlamps. They could be dangerous if you left them on too long. But I didn't plan to do that. I wheeled them over close to the sailor and turned them on. His body showed white as marble under the loosely knit garment of curly black body hair. How beautiful he was! Like some saint undergoing a martyrdom by torture.

I went back to the chest. There were lots of dildos, and I took several in successively larger sizes. I brought them back and rotated him slightly, so that the camera (if there was one) would be able to see what I was doing.

First I slid my index finger up his ass. Then two fingers. Then three, and then four. I wondered if it was possible to slide a whole hand up somebody's ass; but it seemed to me that it might kill a person. I pulled my fingers out, then slowly put in the first dildo and started working it in and out.

He was already over the edge from the restraints. I wasn't sure whether using a dildo on him would be considered sexual or not, but it occurred to me that a lot of what the corporal wanted was to see me horny and unsatisfied, so I took a chance and fucked the sailor by proxy with a rubber penis.

I got him going with the first one, then took it out and inserted a slightly larger one. The blazing lights close to his body were making him sweat profusely, so he glistened and dripped; and the sweat fell on my bare body and ran down the dildo onto my hand. It was as if he were coming out of his pores, spattering his vital essences on me in the only way he could, just as I was making love to him in the only way I could. I moved the dildo faster, faster, then, on a back thrust, slid it out and slid in an even larger one.

He shrieked. A thrill went through me. It was the first time anyone had ever screamed as I thrust into them. It didn't matter that it wasn't my cock. Not even the few girls I'd screwed when I was younger had ever shrieked. I moved the tool faster, becoming delirious with the pleasure of what I was doing.

He twisted, hanging there in the air. He thrashed about, trying to escape the battering I was giving him. But there was no escape. He could buck away, but gravity swung him back onto it every time.

I pulled it out and put in another, bigger one.

"No! *No!*" he began to scream.

I wondered if I was really going too far. I wondered if they had set me up to do him some real damage. But I was out of control, and these thoughts didn't impinge very hard on my consciousness. I fucked him savagely, wanting to make the Marines in the movie look like amateurs. I wanted them to look at what I was doing and wish they could do as well.

And I wanted the boy I was fucking to come! I needed it, I demanded it. He *would* come if I had to fuck him so hard my arm fell off! I yanked the dildo I was using out of him and shoved in another, yet bigger one.

And that was it.

As it went in he screamed, a long, piercing scream, and his body jerked; and slowly, through his tightly bound prick, the orgasm erupted. Just like in the movie, only with his cock tied shut, very slowly and painfully, taking a long, long time. Drop by drop his huge load came out, one sticky gob after another dripping from the swollen purple head and flinging here and there, some even spattering on me as he jerked back and forth.

I wanted desperately to take that slowly seeping organ into my mouth and suck it dry. I wanted to lick the sweat from his body and let him slump into my arms. But I stood there, slowing the pumping of the dildo up his ass, until by the time he had stopped coming, it was barely moving. Then I let it out.

I stood breathing hard. I had done what they had told me to do. I was sweating as hard as he was. But I hadn't come off. I still stood with a hard cock, quaking with lust for the exhausted sailor who hung above me.

I looked up at him, hanging there, still now. I wanted him so desperately. I wanted him more than for sex, but sex was what I wanted first. Yet I had done for him what I could not do for myself. I hoped that he understood that.

A voice cracked through the panting quiet of the room.

"Get him down and see if he's still alive!"

Suddenly the stillness of him hanging there was not just quiet, it was ominous. My desire was traded instantly for fear. Had I killed him?

I dashed for the rope and lowered him to the floor.

He didn't move. His eyes were closed. I ran to him, feeling something inside me that was worse than fear, worse than anything I'd ever felt. I fell down beside him and put my ear to his chest, felt for his pulse.

What I had done? *What had I done?*

Then, finally, I heard it. His heart was beating! I found his pulse. It was pounding. It was unnatural and almost syncopated, but it was there.

He was alive.

I threw my arms around him. I kissed his face, his eyelids. I started laughing and crying.

The door opened, but I didn't look up. I didn't care what they did to me.

He was alive!

"Hadn't you better take off the restraints?" I heard the dark corporal say, and there was amused contempt in his voice. "That thing on his cock could give him gangrene if it stays on much longer. Then the doc would have to cut his dick off!"

Sixteen

They told me that I had failed my test. That I had started telling the black-haired sailor how much I loved him as I took off the 'Seven Gates of Hell' and the tit clamps. I tried to say that that was just a part of the Big Lie, but then they told me I was talking back, something a dog must never do.

They told me I would have to be punished severely. Then they took me back to my cell, and presumably they took the sailor back to his. I wondered next morning how he was. I felt something deep for him, but I wondered too whether it was love or something momentary, something induced by manipulation. Nothing was sure any more. Everything was subject to doubt. It might be that the sailor was a set-up. It might be that his passing out at the end was something they could count on, an effect designed to bring about my complete capitulation, just as it had.

But I remembered the look in his eyes as he awoke, lying there in my arms on the floor. I didn't believe that the black-haired, brown eyed sailor was a lie. He might have been inserted into the scenario as a ruse with full knowledge of what he could and could not take, but I was sure from the look that he gave me as he awoke in my arms that he had not been a willing participant in any scheme to manipulate me. He was just as much a victim as I was.

Moreover, I was sure from that look he gave me out of his beautiful brown eyes that he had at last understood that I loved him, for what it was worth.

I was a long time in my cell alone. Time had ceased to be real. My body rhythms were gone, or at least under my captor's control. It could have been only a day; it could have been several days. They didn't give me any food, and they didn't take me out. I recognized this as a build-up for some new torture, but it didn't particularly inspire me to fear. Nothing can make you afraid when you have nearly killed someone you love. Not for a while, at least.

When they finally came it was just one of them: the redhead, the country boy. The bright and healthy image of young America, the boy who just

reeked apple pie and Mom and the flag, and who probably set fire to cats for
fun.

He smiled all the while he led me through the halls. He kept smiling as
he scalded me in the shower. I wondered if he would be more comfortable
with a straw in his mouth as he led me to yet another section of the prison
that I had never visited. I could see him with a pitchfork, standing next to
a hay rick, or next to a sulfur pit!

The room to which he took me was filled with electronic gear. There were
dials and switches in banks around the room, and I felt flashes of mad
scientists run across my brain.

In the middle of the room was a bed, a very large one, covered with only
a plain white sheet. A square metal rim ran around the mattress, and was
attached by chains to pulleys on the ceiling. The chains went through the
pulleys and disappeared into the smooth, acoustical ceiling, so I assumed
they were operated by machines rather than muscle. The set-up was quite
elaborate, and I figured they could move the frame into any position they
chose. At the top and bottom of the frame there were smaller chains, attached
at one end to ratchets on the frame and at the other to sets of padded
manacles.

"You just lie down there," said the redhead. "Face down and spread-
eagle."

I did as I was told, and after a minute or two I heard a door open. Someone
else came into the room, and I felt the manacles fastened on my wrists and
ankles. Then I heard the little ratchets on the frame operate and I was
stretched out tight, spread-eagled.

More machinery sounded and the frame started to lift. I was brought
upright, facing the bed, and I could see the other person in the room. He was
a man in his late thirties, wearing a white lab coat, with iron grey hair at his
temples and a hard-as-iron, handsome sort of face. He looked like a family
doctor, but the cold set of his mouth was not something to inspire trust. He
was adjusting gadgets at some kind of control board to my left; and as I came
straight up, he flicked a switch that stopped my movement.

He wheeled a little table over to me, a kind of cart, connected to the electronic equipment by a long, complex length of cable. There were dozens of wires on the table and some bottles.

Without ever looking at me, he began attaching the wires to my body. A little bit of glue from one of the bottles, the wire stuck into it, then a little white bandage over it. The glue was cold, but it warmed after a minute, and I figured it was probably comfortable compared to what they were going to do to me next.

The wires were attached all over. To my toes, up the inside of my legs, on the backs of my knees, to my testicles, to my penis; one special one stuck up my ass, and somehow attached inside with a painful probe of his fingers. Up my sides, on my belly, to my nipples, along my arms. One to each of my fingers, some on my neck, a couple on my face, my lips, my ears, and two that really bothered me, on my eyelids.

It took a long time; but he finally finished, and I was wired up. The 'mad scientist' stepped back, checking me over. He nodded.

"There's a screen on the wall over there," he said, his voice as cold as his smile. He indicated the wall opposite me. "There'll be a lot of pictures on it for the next few hours, and you're going to look at them. The process you're going to be put through is called aversion therapy, and it's for your own good, as well as the country's. You'll be seeing a lot of pictures of things that men normally like, and a lot of pictures of things that men don't normally like. When an image comes on the screen that we want you to shy away from in the future, you'll receive a painful shock; like this."

He flicked a switch and an agonizing pain ran up my arm, down my chest, to my tit. I groaned. The pain lasted only a second, but it was horrible. Anyone who has ever had an electric shock can imagine what it was like, but not the fear that came with it. I realized that he could send shocks throughout my body between any two of the terminals he'd attached to me!

"When you see an image we want you to respond favorably to, we'll give you a different kind of stimulation."

He flipped another switch, and something else happened. It was another kind of shock, but it was applied in a different way, or to a different kind of nerve in my body. My cock grew instantly hard. I felt a tingle in my ass. Lust washed over me like a flood.

He smiled.

There wasn't even the vicious humanity of the redhead in his smile. It was a smile, not for my reaction, but for the dependability of his equipment!

"I won't have to stay and control it, Corporal," he said to the redhead. "It's all run by computer from here on. You know what to do when the screen goes blank at the end. Just ring the bell when you're finished with him, and I come in and disengage the machinery."

He went out, and shut the door behind him. The corporal walked slowly over and stood in front of me, his face directly before my hard cock. He smiled up at me. Then he leaned a little forward, opened his mouth, and started to lick the underside of my cock head. Following the stimulation the machine had given me, it was exquisite. I felt myself rush toward orgasm. But he stopped, as I knew he would.

He walked over to the bank of dials in the wall and moved his hand ever so slowly toward a big red button. I knew that it was the button that would set things in motion. He knew that I knew it, and he relished the tension as I waited for his finger to make contact. His finger hovered over the button for a long time, then he asked: "Do you love me, Rover? The way you love that sailor?"

"Sir! Yes, Sir!" I responded.

He punched the button.

I don't know what I had expected. Perhaps a picture and then a shock. But it wasn't like that at all. It was fast, horrendously fast. There would be a picture on the screen, then the shock or the stimulation, then another picture and another stimulation, but it happened ten or twenty times per second!

The data was going into my brain faster than I could think about it. If I could have thought that fast it wouldn't have mattered, because the change from pain to pleasure was so rapid I didn't have time to do anything but feel. And I felt as I had never felt before. Pain that shocked through me from point to point. From nipple to arm. From toe to testicle. Instantaneous pain! And pleasure that surged through me just as fast and just as diverse.

But there was an illogic to it!

I suppose I had expected them to show me pictures of girls, and give me shocks, then pictures of boys and give me pleasure. I had expected the therapy to be used to make me more queer. But it wasn't that simple.

They already had me where they wanted as far as my orientation. Now they wanted my responses narrowed. I would see pictures of two men kissing, and I would be given a shock, from my toe right up my leg and out my balls. Then I would be shown a man being beaten by two cops, and I would be given the pleasure.

I found myself shrieking at comforts and turned on by terrors. It was just more of what they'd been doing all along, but it was faster and more intense; and it was not only turning me on to pain, it was turning me off to tenderness.

I thought about the love I'd felt for the black-haired sailor, the feeling of warmth, the desire to touch and comfort him. *That* was what they were ripping out of me. That was what they were making impossible for me!

I started to hate!

Not the slight, fragile emotion that is gone when the anger that inspires it goes, but the deep, glowing hatred that lasts for a lifetime and fires revolutions. A hatred that burns all the way down at the center where the wellsprings of human kindness have dried up. And the hatred ran in harness with the lust!

Cock and balls and tits and arms, anguish and pain and brutality and desire. My feelings were racehorses running at full tilt. The sweat poured off my soul as the shocks ran through my body. I was afraid of love. I was in love with hate!

How long it went on I don't know. It must have been forever, because it did its job. When the lights went out on the screen and the lights came up in the room, I was still there, stretched spread-eagle, and my body didn't feel any different. But my insides felt a lot different.

The corporal came over to me and again looked at my hard dick. Again he opened his mouth and leaned close, and started to lick the underside.

But this time it wasn't good; it was agony. It was as if someone were scraping it with sandpaper.

He reached up and grabbed hold of my balls, hard, and twisted them. I should have screamed. Instead, I moaned with pleasure.

He stepped back and laughed. Then he went over and pushed another button. I didn't hear any bell ring, but I figured that must be what it was. A minute later the grey-haired scientist came in.

"Almost finished, Doc," the corporal said. "I just got a couple more things I want to do with him, if you'll trust me to unhook him from the frame. I just want to fuck him, you know."

The Doc smiled that cold smile and began taking the wires off me. Never once did he give me any more attention than he would have given a piece of machinery. It was as if my face were another gadget to be played with!

All the wires came off and he lowered the metal frame. I was once again spread-eagled, face down on the bed, stretched taut. The doctor left.

There was a long silence, and I remembered the savagery with which the redhead had handled me in the past. The whipping, the slapping. I began to grow harder, anticipating his assault with delight.

"Poor Rover," he said gently, and I felt his hand caress my back.

It was the ultimate torture. I felt revulsion at his gentleness. I felt my cock start to soften.

"Everyone has been so rough on you all this time," he continued. There wasn't even a trace of cynicism to hang on to! "But now it will all be different. I'm going to take real good care of you. I'm going to be gentle and kind. I'm going to fuck you better, and nicer, than you've ever been fucked before."

I turned my face to the side of the bed where he was. I watched as he slowly stripped. Even the way he took his clothes off was different. He expressed kindness in his every gesture. He looked now like the kind of boy who goes to Sunday School till he's twenty, rather than the kind who pulls turtles out of their shells.

How much of this is him, and how much me? I wondered. Is it the conditioning, or is he really acting differently?

He lay down beside me. His smooth, naked body was beautiful, and I was repelled by it. The way I would have been repelled if it had happened before I entered the Brig. I saw him suddenly as a faggot, about to abuse my body. I saw him as something alien.

His freckled face, his smooth, freckled chest. His corded muscles, his leanness. The thick, crinkly patch of pubic hair around his cock, redder, but stiffer than the hair on his head. His long, thin cock, with its head bigger than the shaft, its big purple shiny head sliding wetly up out of the foreskin.

He started to softly stroke my back. I shivered. His hand went down and toyed gently with my ass. He played with the little patch of hair that was grown back in above the crack. His finger slid smoothly into my asshole. I trembled with fear as if I'd never been fucked before!

He began kissing my shoulders, and the back of my neck, and then he slowly rolled over on top of me. I was shaking with fear.

"Sir!" I began to plead. "Please, Sir! Hurt me, Sir! Please do something to hurt me!"

I felt his mouth at my ear.

"No, baby," he crooned. "Nobody is ever gonna hurt you again."

I felt him slide his cock into my ass, slowly, gently, lovingly. I tried to clamp down on it with my ass muscles, to do anything that would get a response out of him. But I was spread-eagled, and I didn't have half the control over my body that I needed.

He started to fuck me, very gently, sliding in and out, and I felt his hands roam gently over my body. My cock was completely soft now, and I trembled with fear and revulsion at what was happening to me. Had the aversion therapy been so successful, so complete?

He put his arms around me and began to slowly massage my nipples. Yesterday it would have been wonderful. Now I wanted him to pinch, to twist. I started to beg him, to plead with him. I felt like the old joke about the masochist and the sadist; the sadist is the one who says 'no' when the masochist begs to be beaten.

He took his time fucking me, letting me crumble completely under his gentleness. I was blubbering helplessly by the time he was ready to shoot his load. But then his true self just had to exert itself, and he'd planned for that moment anyway.

"I just love fucking you," he whispered into my ear, his rhythm increasing as he slid his rod in and out of me. "Gently, ever so gently. Just the way I fucked that girl the last couple of nights. Oh, you should have heard her squeal. Man, I fucked her good. Like she'd never been fucked before. Certainly like you never fucked her."

I started.

"Man, them Catholic bitches, them Puerto Rican girls, they really know how to lose their virginity! You know, baby? But no, you don't know, 'cause you never got into her pants. She told me that, right after I showed her the movie of you in the pretty dress. And man, did she cry when she saw what kind of guy you really were, doing all that stuff to the sailor. Jeez, but those guys know how to make movies!"

He was fucking real fast now, and I wanted to kill him. But I was chained and helpless.

"Oh, man, was she ever ready to get fucked."

He was panting.

"Your little *fiancee!*" he snarled, and I felt him shoot it up my ass.

And at last, I enjoyed it!

Seventeen

I ate my breakfast the next morning and sat staring at the wall of my cell. What had I become?

My dreams had been confused, erratic. There had been visions of my life before the Navy: the seminary, my parents, the girls I'd fucked. The parts about the girls and the fucking had forced me awake in a cold sweat of fear. They weren't wet dreams, they were nightmares!

And there had been visions of boys and men.

I've learned since that this kind of dream is a classic among gay men when they finally come out. All the little secret wishes are brought to the surface of the mind and finally confronted. The kids that you grew up with, that you watched when they took a piss in the woods. The boys in the shower in high school. The fascination with somebody else's erection that you always thought to be no more than comparison.

The part of a man that is homosexual is there from very early in life, just as the part that is heterosexual is there. The attractions are natural, normal as far as Mother Nature goes. It is only the repressions of society that bend and twist natural desire, and make it into something ugly. It is that twisting that makes men tell queer jokes in the bathroom, never understanding that bathroom jokes are just bedroom jokes they don't want to face squarely.

When a man tells a queer joke, he is taking something inside himself and trying to put it outside. Like putting out the cat at night, because its meowing keeps you awake. Most men not only put it out, they try and put it in someone else's back yard! But the cat always comes back. And because a cat has nine lives, and you only have one, you can never kill the cat. You'll still feel it whining inside you.

Some men feel it so strongly and are such cowards about facing it, that they come to hate those who can face it. They go around bashing queers, trying to destroy in others what they have come to loathe in themselves. It's the same mechanism that makes the ugly hate the beautiful, the cowardly hate the brave, and the evil undermine the good, never realizing that the beauty, the bravery, and the goodness have been purchased with hard work, not inherited from providence.

My visions troubled me, and I had to reason it all out. Had I been homosexual all along? The visions of the guys in high school and the excitement I felt when I thought about them, made me think so. But what about the girls? I hadn't been repulsed by them when I had fucked them. That was new, that revulsion. That, I knew, was a result of my incarceration. Was it possible that a man could want both?

I know now that it is possible, though unusual, in a society that puts such rigid barriers between gay and straight. If I had grown up in a world where it was usual, who knows? I might have continued to want women, even after being forced 'out' in the Brig. As it is, I don't. I no longer derive any satisfaction from them sexually.

I know, because I've tried.

But that day, sitting on my cot, I didn't know anything for sure.

Well, no. I did know some things for sure.

I knew that I wanted to be hurt. I knew that pain turned me on, and that affection turned me off.

And that scared me.

After I had eaten several meals, my sergeant came to me.

I thought of him now as 'my' sergeant. There were other sergeants all over the Brig, but this one was special. He was my keeper, my trainer, and, in a very special sense, my lover. It is a relationship the military knows how to cultivate and which it always does cultivate between young men and their officers. It is this sexual tension, usually kept under strict repression, that makes for the absolute and unquestioning loyalty necessary to militarism in general. Without it, it would be impossible for nations to raise armies and enter into wars. Empires are not built without power, and the greatest power in mankind is sexual: harness it completely and you can own men's minds and maybe the world.

I rose and started to get down on my knees to assume a proper posture for a dog and a worshipper.

"You're finished," my sergeant said, quietly and evenly.

I didn't understand him.

"Tonight is your last night in the Brig. Your eight weeks are finished. Tomorrow you'll get your discharge from the service."

I froze, half-way down on my knees. I had heard this song before, from the lips of the dark corporal. It had been a lie then; why should it be anything else now?

My sergeant started to strip.

"I'm going to give you a little going-away present," he said as he took off his clothes. "Something you haven't had before and something you won't get again."

I watched entranced as he folded his clothes neatly and laid them on the floor, next to the door. I devoured the beauty of his body as he uncovered it! His broad, thickly muscled chest, covered with a pelt of black, curly hair; his rounded biceps; his thick forearms, so powerful when he wielded a belt!

His narrow waist; his tight, hard ass. His columns of legs, prickly with that curly black hair. The way the hair thickened below his navel and grew tight as a rug around his thick, dark cock and his big, pendulous balls.

He even took off his boots and stood before me, his legs spread wide, his big balls hanging down between them, his cock already halfway up. Totally naked.

A shock of black hair fell across his forehead, very casual, very unmilitary. His black eyes gleamed, and his mouth curved in a broad, proud smile. He put his fists on his hips and stood, arms akimbo, letting me worship him.

"You're just what I want you to be," he almost whispered after a little while. "Much less than a man. Much less than a slave. Less than a dog."

I felt his words sting, because I knew they were true.

"From now on," he continued, "you won't even be able to get it up, unless someone whips you. And if somebody is willing to whip you, then they're going to take their satisfaction from you; and you'll get what they give you, and no questions asked. You may never get a chance at the active role in sex again. You'll probably never fuck anybody again for as long as you live. So tonight, for the first time in your life, you're going to fuck a man. Just so you'll always know what you're missing."

His words were like swords, and they plunged all the way to my heart. I felt them to be absolutely true. The fear I'd thought was a thing of the past came back.

"Stand up," he said gently.

I did as I was told. He came to me and wrapped his powerful arms around me, and I felt his hairy body close against me, his hard cock against my belly. I lay my head on his broad chest. He stroked my hair. Then he knelt and took my cock in his mouth, and started to suck it.

And I went completely soft.

I started to shake all over as the horror of what has was happening finally hit me. I started to cry, to sob uncontrollably, and finally I staggered back, pulling my limp prick from between his lips.

"You bastard," I shouted between sobs. "You bastard! I can't get it up! I can't get it up unless you hurt me, you son of a bitch!"

He came to his feet and his smile opened wider and wider and he started to laugh. His triumph was complete.

"You're right," he said. "You can't get it up unless I whip you. But I will whip you, don't worry. After all, you deserve a nice going-away present. You've been so easy for me. You've broken so nicely. You didn't have the guts that half my prisoners have! I'll give you all the pity I've got, because you deserve it!"

With that he drew his arm back and slapped me across the face, hard. Then he went to his clothes and drew the belt from his trousers.

"Lie down on your bed!" he commanded.

I lay down, my face stinging, but somehow, miraculously, the fear ebbing away. I lay on my face, anxiously awaiting the first blow.

It came, across my ass.

Thwack!

"Got it hard yet?" he asked.

"Sir! No, Sir!"

"How many more do you want?"

"As many as you want, Sir!"

He landed another, across my ass. I felt the blood pouring into my cock, the hardness rushing in.

Thwack!

It didn't take long for me to get hard as a rock, but I didn't want him to stop whipping me. It was what I wanted more than anything! The pain was wonderful, like stars bursting inside my flesh.

Thwack!

He stopped, shoved his hand in under my belly, and felt my hard cock.

"Get up!" he commanded.

I got up, my prick stiff as a ship's mast.

He lay down, face up, on my rack.

"Lie down here, on top of me!" he said.

I did so, feeling the warm hairiness of his body once again against the whole length of me. My hard cock nestled against the thick bush of his lower belly. I felt his big, hard prick slide between my legs and push up against my balls.

He took my wrists in his powerful grip, one in each hand, and twisted my arms behind me in a double nelson. My arms ached with the pain, but I wanted it. My face was only inches from his. His breath, strong with cigarette smoke, entered my open mouth and filled my lungs. It was like a new kind of sexual violation.

"You're gonna fuck me," he whispered, close to my face. "You're gonna fuck me real good! And after that you're gonna suck me, and suck me real good. And after that there won't be anything in the world left for you!"

He twisted my arms harder, and I felt his legs slide apart, so that my legs fell between them. He released my arms and lifted my hips, so that his prick fell upward, flat against his own belly, out from between my legs. Then he slid his legs upward along my sides, and put his knees over my shoulders. I was forced away from his chest by his strong thighs, and my cock now lay along the open crack of his ass.

"Come on," he said. "Shove it in!"

I reached down and positioned the head of my cock against the pucker of his asshole. He reached up between his thighs and took my nipples between his thumbs and forefingers.

"Come on!" he said, pinching.

I pushed, and the head of my cock parted the warm tightness and pushed in a little.

"Harder!" he said.

I shoved, and my shaft went in half way. For the first time I had penetrated a man's ass!

"I said *fuck me*!" my sergeant snarled, and twisted my tits like hell.

And I shoved it in all the way!

And everything seemed to change.

He was hard and warm and tight inside. His ass grasped my cock as tight as ever my own fist could. The pain of my tits became one with the pleasure of my hard cock, and my hard cock was suddenly a weapon, deep inside my enemy's body.

I pulled back, almost all the way out, and rammed it in, hard! All the way to the hilt.

He grunted, and twisted my tits again.

And suddenly I understood the game.

It was like wrestling, or war. We were going to fight one another. He was going to hurt me, and I was going to give it back with my prick.

And man, did I ever want to give it back.

He twisted again, and I started to ram him, fucking like I had never fucked before, using my tool like a battering ram. I was going to kill him with my cock!

I wrapped my arms around his legs, getting better leverage, holding him down as I shoved it in, harder and harder. I looked down at him, and saw the intensity of pleasure on his face. And I saw something else, too.

I saw my own reflection in his black eyes, eyes shiny as mirrors.

My own face was just like his! Hard and intense and powerful as I fucked him. I wasn't like a slave or a dog. I was like a man. Like my sergeant, like the two corporals. There was no submissiveness in my face now, only raw power. Only pure lust!

And as I saw that, reflected in the twin mirrors of his eyes, I saw a change come over me. All the things that had happened to me were resolved. I had been a slave, a dog, a prisoner. But right now, as I fucked my sergeant, I was a Ma*ster!*

He saw the change, too.

And his face changed, also.

The mask of mastery began to crack. He knew, suddenly that he was no longer in charge!

"All right," he said. "That's enough! You didn't think you were really going to get it all, did you?"

But the tone of absolute power was thin. Too thin to force my responses. And big as he was, I was on top and in him.

I smiled, seeing my smile's reflection, and his mask shattered. He started to panic.

"You heard me!" he commanded. "That's enough!"

"Sir! Yes, Sir!" I responded, but the value of the words was changed. They dripped with the same powerful poisons that he had always used to enervate me. And I didn't pull out. I started to fuck him harder.

He twisted my tits as hard as he could, but it felt good. It was his counteroffensive to my assault, and I already knew what it felt like; it felt like my prick getting stiffer!

He let go of my tits, anger blazing in his eyes, and reached up to push me off. But his hands never got to my shoulders. I grabbed his wrists and forced them back, pinned them above his head, where he couldn't bring his muscles into play. He was stronger than I was, but he didn't have eight weeks of hell sitting inside him!

He tried to use his strong legs to push me off, but I expected it. He was doubled in half. I had the advantage. I fucked him harder, using the strength of my hips, thrusting in. I tried to rip him wide open. I rammed him from another angle, and held him pinned as he yelped.

"Goddamn it, get off!" he tried to command, but it was gone out of him to command by that point.

"Aren't you forgetting something?" I asked, using my cock to hurt him, to make him suffer. "What about 'Sir'?"

He struggled but I had him.

"Come on!" I snarled, "As of now, I outrank you, Sergeant! "

And in his black eyes, those beautiful black eyes like black mirrors, he shattered.

"Sir!" he snapped. "Sir! Yes, Sir!"

I felt the tingling in my balls. I was going to come!

"You want me to come?" I sneered.

"Sir! Yes, Sir!"

"Beg for it!"

"Please, Sir! Shoot it up my ass, Sir! Come, Sir!"

The volcano inside blew.

Hot lava came boiling up, molten magma out of my balls, through my groin, out of my cock, shooting hard into the sergeant's ass. Deep down inside him, spewing out in the hot inside of him, filling him with my semen, making a part of me part of him, and making him *mine*. I shot with a force such as I had never known, and it went on and on, filling him up, possessing him, leaving him no more than a receptacle for my pleasure. He was now what I had been.

And he knew it.

I could see it in his eyes.

We didn't speak after that.

When I was finished with him, he got up and dressed, and left silently. I felt kind of hollow inside myself, because when something in him was shattered, something in me shattered too. It's not easy to see your idols crumble, from their clay feet upward.

I wondered, much later that night, whether it was indeed my last night in the Brig. Whether or not tomorrow would show me a sergeant with renewed confidence and ingenuity.

Eighteen

The men who came for me in the morning were strangers. A sergeant and two corporals, as usual; they brought with them my uniform for the Brig and took me through a routine that was the reverse of the one I'd been through upon entering.

I didn't wonder about my sergeant or his two corporals. I knew instinctively that I would not see them again. They were through with me. And I was through with them.

I got my shower, the first one in an eternity that wasn't scalding. (I almost waited for them to turn the faucet for me!) Then I got a second set of shorts, dungarees, socks, and a shirt stenciled 'Brig'.

The games were still going, I thought. But it didn't really bother me. If this time around was a lie, like the other time, then so be it: I could stand being a slave; I could even enjoy it. I had proved what else I was to the only person who counted: myself!

They marched me to the room with the strongboxes, and I got back everything that was mine, including my clothes. I suppose it was that that finally convinced me. The time they'd lied about my release, they'd given me my uniform in my cell. Now everything was going, once again, according to regulations.

We left the Brig, and I saw that the weather had changed. There was a touch of autumn in the air and even a little color here and there among the maples. No wonder the nights had been cold, I thought. And then I asked myself, what nights? I think I was a little dazed.

We didn't drive to a ship, and that surprised me at first and put fear back into me. But then I realized that we couldn't go back to my ship. She'd been set to sail within two weeks when I was imprisoned; that was why they were taking me to a Navy administration building instead.

We went through corridors, and it seemed to me that things in the administration building were not much different than they were in the Brig. No bright colors, no pictures on the wall, except the big one in the lobby of the President, between two flags. It was as if the very act of being in the service were a kind of penalty.

Why did they doom men to this dreariness? I wondered. Why didn't they make things brighter for the men who defended the country? They were always complaining about how necessary the draft was; it was no wonder they didn't get volunteers when they made things so unpleasant.

The absurdity of my thought processes trickled down over my brain like cool water. Had I learned nothing about the military in my eight weeks' imprisonment?

I realized that my ardent, and foolish, pacifism had been something on the surface. I had been outraged by the napalm we were throwing at babies. I had not seen to the greater heart of darkness that produced all wars and miseries among mankind.

Of course they doomed sailors and soldiers and marines and airmen to dreariness! They also manipulated their sexuality and everything else necessary to maintain control.

And so did the Russians. And the Chinese. And whoever else was running a nation anywhere in time and space. Unless somewhere, in the far reaches of space, someone had found a better way.

I was marched into an office, and there was another picture of the President. Our symbol of trust! There was the flag. Our symbol of loyalty! And there was a desk, with an officer behind it, and here was I, saluting: poorly, from lack of practice.

A dog, after all, looks silly saluting.

There was another man in the office, and he looked strangely familiar. He wore civilian clothes, very conservative, and had wavy hair that was fading from red to grey. I couldn't quite place him, but I kept trying to as they asked me a series of ritual questions, tried to get me to renege on my request for a discharge, and finally let me sign the papers that released me.

When I was officially discharged (honorably), the man with the red-grey hair spoke, and I knew who he was: Congressman Hal Rosenblum.

"Young man," he said, addressing me. "I want to apologize to you for what has happened on behalf of the Congress and the People of the United States of America."

I stood, dumbfounded.

The officer in charge had a sour look about his mouth. The sergeant and two corporals saluted and left the room, as if they didn't want to hear what was coming next.

"It is a rare abuse, I am sure, but that doesn't excuse it," he continued. "No officer in any of the United States Armed Services has any right to hold up a discharge."

I stared at him.

"Hold up a discharge?" I asked.

"Yes," he said. "Didn't they tell you?"

I shook my head.

"Your commanding officer aboard your ship had your discharge in hand nearly eight weeks ago. Instead of putting it through, he held on to it. If it hadn't been for that letter you wrote to me, you might never have got out of the Brig! But don't you worry; I'm pressing for a full investigation of the matter. This war has brought about too many abuses of privilege on the part of the military, and I'm going to see that it stops. Personally."

And I guess that was when I fainted.

When I woke up, I was in Congressman Rosenblum's hotel room in Boston. He hadn't let them take care of me there at the administration building the way they had offered to; he said he knew something was wrong when he saw it, and wanted to make sure I was safe.

I told him the whole story.

I had never seen a congressman, or any other politician, shocked. I have never seen one since. But Hal Rosenblum was something special in American politics. He was an honest man with ideals and courage, and he was willing to fight for what he felt to be right.

That was why they killed him a week later, on a campaign tour of California.

When I heard about it on the radio, I took all the money I had and bought a Greyhound ticket to a town in Montana that I picked with a map and a dart. I used the map and the dart again and hitchhiked to a place in Kansas. After that I figured out how to dye my hair in the middle of the night and leave before daybreak any place I'd been.

Jobs were short-lived and mainly consisted of sweeping and washing dishes. I had my discharge papers and using them scared me a lot; but after a while I figured out that They weren't looking for me. My one bolt had been shot.

Hitchhiking brought me in contact with truck drivers, and being young and pretty good-looking, it wasn't long before I found out about gay drivers. I found there was a good, cheap way to travel and one that wasn't likely to get me traced.

I ended up in San Francisco, and once the fear had subsided, settled down to sort myself out. After a couple of years I ended up in the bars on Folsom Street, where the leather crowd hangs out, and found that I was not the only man in the world who liked to get hurt while he was coming.

I found that I was an accomplished masochist, and further, that it didn't bother me to be one. I found out that I was gay, and that in San Francisco that was no further down the ladder than being black or a woman. Sure, there was prejudice, but not like what I'd grown up around.

And I started to change.

And the war ended.

And then . . .

Epilogue

It was a long time after.

The war was over.

Oh, not all wars. Just the one in Viet Nam. The long, undeclared war.

And Nixon was over.

And Martin Luther King was dead.

And lots of things had changed, including me.

I was standing in the dark corner of a room with a pool table. One light bulb lit the table, hanging over it in a conical metal shade. Just that, the cone of light, made me think back to the room with the wooden table and the Brig. I probably wouldn't have noticed if it hadn't been for that.

But I did notice, amid the heady smell of beer and urine that is characteristic of all such dives, whether gay or straight. I noticed, and a thrill went through me, a feeling of excitement.

He had changed, but it was him. My sergeant.

There were wrinkles around his eyes, and his skin was a little more leathery than you'd expect, even in a leatherneck. He was standing by the bar in the next room and smiling that slight, cruel smile of his. There was a kid next to him that I knew, a biker, and he was obviously trying to put the make on the kid. I noted that he was wearing black leather now, instead of Marine drag. Maybe he'd got tired of that routine.

I finished my beer and went into the next room, moving through the crowd to the bar, not far from him. I wondered whether he would know me on sight. It didn't matter, but I hoped not. I ordered a Dos Equis and smiled at the kid, whose name was Bill. He smiled back, and my sergeant turned to see who he was smiling at.

There was no recognition in his shiny black eyes.

Good.

I pitched my voice a little lower than usual and introduced myself. It didn't matter, because I hadn't used my real name in years.

He introduced himself to me and, much as I expected, his name too was different.

I've learned a lot about masculine charm and it wasn't difficult to turn it on to him. As we talked, I casually shifted my keys from my left belt-loop to my right, making sure that he noticed it. I had noted right off that he wore his on the left.

He would.

We drank, and Bill drifted away. I knew he would, because Bill has a thing about blondes like me; that's all he goes home with.

The bar closed, and I offered my place, which has a nice game room. My sergeant accepted.

As I said, I've learned a lot over the years.

He followed me up the long flight of stairs at the back of the old, brick factory, and didn't suspect a thing until I had the cuffs on him. He started to protest, telling me he was strictly a topman, but it was too late then. In a matter of minutes I had him strung up, stretched spread-eagled in the center of the room.

Then I turned up the lights, just enough to let him see my face, and told him who I was.

It took him a while to remember me, and that hurt a little. But after all, I had been one of many, perhaps more than a thousand. I was curious about that, and figured I'd find out. There was time.

One of the things I learned from my sergeant, from the two corporals, and from lots of men since, was the use of time. Time allows a bottom to understand what is being done to him, and how. Sufficient time will allow him to become a top, and a good one.

Just how good, I figured I would learn from my (*my!*) sergeant's beautiful, black, captive eyes.

AFTERWORD

What became of the young sailor after his release from the brig? — I think I have made the general pattern clear in the Epilogue, but there are plenty of readers who have asked me, in the ten years since the book's appearance, for a more detailed accounting.

If I were to write a sequel, one thing is certain: I would not model it on Kelson's life. His life was quite different from what I imagine that of the young sailor to be; and I *do* pretty much know what happened to the young sailor because the sequel was fully planned out in my mind the day I finished writing *The Brig*. Someday, if there is incentive, I may write that sequel.

But what became of Kelson between the time he was released from the Brig and his death?

That question, too, has been asked by readers, and, at the request of my publisher, I offer this quick sketch of his all too brief life.

In civilian clothes, Kelson tried to glue the pieces of his life together. He sought out his best friend from high school, who by that point was in the Air Force. They lived together off base for a while as roommates: buddies, nothing more. But it was too much for Kelson. He knew he loved his friend, but he still had no idea how to deal with that love, or accept it.

He had made a kind of sexual contact with another man before this point. In the Brig, after a particularly brutal beating, one of the Marine corporals blew him. But he did not identify that as sexuality so much as molestation. He still had no word for his own feelings, and those feelings were too powerful.

After a time living with his friend he attempted suicide. He was still trying to convince himself he did it because he was a typical Straight

American Boy; one who had been through a Hell that he was not able to put aside and forget.

The suicide attempt damaged the friendship irreparably and Kelson and his friend parted ways.

Eventually Kelson found himself in San Francisco, working as a banquet steward at a major hotel. While he was working there he picked up a book that changed his life. Ever a voracious reader, this one looked like a good book about the Christian life: Gordon Merrick's *The Lord Won't Mind*.

I know it's fashionable these days to look down on Merrick — some of you younger readers may not even have heard of the man who, in the 70's and early 80's, was one of the most popular Gay writers — but at that precise moment in the history of the modern Gay movement, Merrick's romantic novels were vitally important to many young men who were coming to terms with a new kind of open and optimistic Gayness that had no literature. — Most tales of Gay life were filled with unhappiness and death.

To Kelson, Merrick's book came as the water of life. Everything came into perspective for him. All his feelings crystalized and he suddenly *understood* that he was *Gay*.

As often happens—or at any rate happened to young men in cities like San Francisco (well, there *are* no cities like San Francisco) in those heady days before AIDS — Kelson went overboard with his new awareness and acceptance of himself. To make up for what he'd been missing, he took up hustling in his off hours. He didn't need the money, but he figured it would be a quick way to gain the experience he was lacking.

He gained it fast.

I met him a couple of years later, through some friends in the Society for Creative Anachronism, a group then devoted to re-creating the Medieval period. He was the household costumer (he had originally been taught to sew by the aunt who made him the Superman costume he wore as a child to lead the parade on the Fourth of July) and our friends felt we would get along.

"He's the only person we've ever met who talks more than you, and besides, he snuggles up on your arm like a little puppy when he goes to sleep."

It took a while, but we eventually came to love each other. Through me Kelson discovered Science Fiction conventions, which gave him more scope for his costuming. I also introduced him to the world of theater, where he quickly showed his talent with costuming and also became an excellent performer, particularly at comic roles.

He discovered the Eastern Churches (beyond his native Byzantine Catholic) and, in 1983, was ordained to the priesthood he had so wanted from childhood. He then went on, in 1987, to become a Bishop of the New Age Universal Church, MeBasrim. He moved with an ecumenical grace among diverse religious groups, at home as much with Pagans and Witches as he was with the Pope, on the occasion of their one brief meeting.

We lived together for eighteen years, had both good times and bad. We fought, we hurt each other, we took to drink. We got over that, with the help of Alcoholics Anonymous, and we got our act together and bought a house in the country, on top of a mountain. We were just about to move in when Kelson was diagnosed with AIDS.

Every HIV-positive person knows what kind of a blow it is to receive that news. How the news itself, let alone the disease, shatters your world. Some take weeks to recover from it and start to put their lives back together, some take months, some never do. Kelson took the news as an opportunity. By the end of that week he was signed up for a speaking tour, getting the message out about what a terrible thing AIDS was, and how it could be prevented. He worked tirelessly to tell people the truth about the disease: but he never for a moment gave in to the idea that it was *sex* that was bad, or particularly Gay sex that was to blame. It was a very long road he had taken to understand that he was Gay, and he was not about to let anything take away from him the joy that the discovery had given him.

My ex-sailor-lover was a feisty little man. I remember him coming home with a bandaged head one morning: somebody had gotten attacked on Folsom Street by three Gay-bashers with lead pipes and he alone ran to the rescue. The attackers got in a couple of good licks before they ran away, but the day was really his — according to the medics, he probably saved the victim's life.

On another occasion he took on fifteen cops, unable to tell them from the guys who had started to mug him. When I arrived on the scene I thought it was all over for the two of us. But when I got him into the car, raving and dripping with blood, the cop in charge straightened his jaw a little and said, "Sir, when your friend comes out of it, will you ask him not to beat up any more cops?"

Funny, but he always thought he lost fights, even though everybody else thought he won them.

A feisty, gentle man, whose main participation in SM consisted in reading about it and looking at pictures for jerkoff stimulation. He never did come to love being beaten as much as his jailers may have wished he would, though he tried it a few times. He indulged from time to time in light SM games, mainly as a top, but he was afraid of the feelings that might be unleashed, and held back.

And yet he loved my book, *The Brig* which I think, indeed, served to lay to rest some of the ghosts that haunted him. The original manuscript became his personal copy. He treasured it, and made much pleasant, private use of it. Once the pain had been put down on the page it became transmogrified, changed; it was taken out of his life and made, in his view, into art. It had *purpose.*

Sailor, priest, poet, cook, costumer, metal worker, actor. He was so many men! In his heavy leather jacket encrusted with chain mail epaulets and pink triangles, with his priests's collar, he was, quite simply, the best *man* I've ever known.

—Mason Powell, June 29th, 1995